Enjoy The adventure !

TEN SILVER COINS

THE DRYLINGS OF ACCHORA

ANDREW KOOMAN

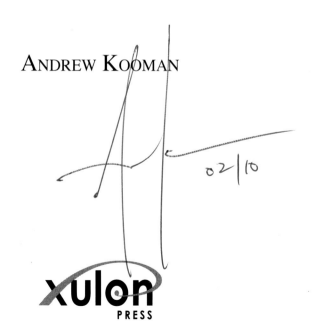

02/10

xulon PRESS

Copyright © 2009 by Andrew Kooman

Ten Silver Coins
The Drylings of Acchora
by Andrew Kooman

Printed in Malaysia

ISBN 9781615793044

All rights reserved solely by the author. The author guarantees all contents are original and do not infringe upon the legal rights of any other person or work. No part of this book may be reproduced in any form without the permission of the author. The views expressed in this book are not necessarily those of the publisher.

Visit **www.tensilvercoins.com** for exciting new content and all the latest Jill Strong news.

Visit **www.andrewkooman.com** to keep up to date with Andrew's latest news, work, and writing.

Artist Photo by Tanya Lee of Eden Photography
Cover Design by Chad Corman

www.xulonpress.com

for my father,
teller of bedtime stories

Or what woman having ten silver coins, if she loses one of them does not light a lamp, sweep the house, and search carefully until she finds it?

Chapter One

The dirt path Jill ran down was overgrown with weeds and thistles. Jill's breathing was laboured from the sprint. She was tired and felt she could run no longer, but was propelled down the path by her caretaker's words. They drew her down the path despite the fatigue that strained her limbs and made them feel like heavy weights. He spoke in the same tone he always used with her, but she could see in his eyes that he was worried, even frantic. *We're not safe Jill, you must run. Run for the Forest!*

The Forest. Jill shuddered. The Forest was the last place she would think of to find safety. The Council warned it was a wicked place. Anyone caught approaching it received harsh punishment, without exception. She would have argued with her caretaker, but his eyes told her to make no objection, told her how serious he was. Nothing made sense, she did not understand the danger, but it was clear, no matter what she thought before, the Forest was the only place safe enough for her to run.

Jill felt like she would explode. She felt like she was holding her breath in a tunnel under water, kicking, pulling, needing to do everything in her power to get to the tunnel's end so she could rush to the surface for air. She had not experienced fear like this in a long time, even in the nightmares that had recently plagued her. And Jill knew if she stopped, if she didn't make it to the end of the tunnel, she would never fill her lungs with a deep breath of fresh air again. She needed to run to the Forest before she could rest, think, breathe.

If she was seen on the road by the Watchmen, they would stop her, detain her, then take her to the mines, a place where she would likely never see her caretaker again, or anyone else willing to show the slightest act of kindness to her, a place where any hope of learning about her family, her history, would die. The path was dark; there were no lights or signs of life on it. Jill could make out the dark, looming presence of trees in the distance. Behind her was the outline of houses and buildings on the edge of the city of Vendor.

Jill could not look back, could not steal one look at the city until she was far within the boundaries of the Forest. Though she knew the city's skyline would soon be illuminated by a series of orange fires billowing in different neighbourhoods, she ran.

The Watchmen and their men, arsons and spies, would be busy setting fires, and their attention would be inside the city, at least for the moment.

They were not fools to think someone would be desperate enough to run to the Forest. *That arrogance will be your salvation, Jill. And my consolation. I will lose all my worldly possessions tonight, maybe even my own life. But you will be safe. If I don't die, I and the book will disappear. We may not see each other again, at least, not for a very long time.*

Jill could still feel the warm kiss from her caretaker's lips on her cheek. It burrowed into her skin, into her blood, helped her along the path in the cool night. Her quiet, mysterious caretaker. Her brave, foolish caretaker! She knew so little about him. He was kind to her though he didn't have to be. Kind to her though he should not have been. She was not always sure he was good, but all this time he held her mother's book! Hid it away somehow, and from the Council. Jill could make no sense of it.

Jill was careful to keep her eye on the path, for it was narrow and uneven, with rocks and stones all about. The path cut through a large meadow. As a little girl, when her mother was still alive, before the Council had risen to power in the city of Vendor, Jill had played in the meadow and even walked along the path. She could remember staring up and making shapes of the white puffs of cloud in the sky. Even as she ran she could smell wildflowers and clover, and imagined hearing the distinct sound of honeybees between gusts of summer breeze from other times.

The closer Jill came to the Forest, the bigger it seemed. The trees on the outskirts of the wood looked bigger and older than the trees in Vendor. Jill slowed to a walk and tried to quiet her breathing. Vendor was now far behind her and she was starting to come upon the boundary of the Forest. Jill hated the thought of being alone at night in an unfamiliar environment, and of all places, the Forest.

When the moon broke through the clouds, Jill started to hesitate, to wonder if her caretaker might have exaggerated the danger of their situation. The trees before her looked metallic and alive. A thick veil of mist shrouded the bottom of the trees. Wisps of mist swirled about the ground like long white fingers, as though the Forest was inviting Jill to enter, if she dare.

Suddenly a siren sounded. Jill turned and looked in the direction of Vendor. Great yellow lights shone in the distance, swept the meadow and the path. Jill heard shouts of *Alarm! Alarm! Someone is on the path!* then watched as one long beam of light slowly, like a giant flashlight, shone down the night sky, searching, seeking, moving toward her as the moon disappeared behind the clouds again. From under the leaves of a fern, Jill watched as the yellow searchlight reached the edge of the Forest and shone directly on the spot Jill, only seconds earlier, had been standing.

Without another thought, Jill had pushed through the low lying wall of mist and entered the Forest as the beam of light swept towards her, heeding her caretaker's words, hoping for safety. She sat motionless until the yellow lights of the Watchmen gave up their search for the lost citizen

of Vendor who ran to the Forest. Tears swelled
in Jill's eyes as she saw the first flames lash into
the sky from one of the northern neighbourhoods.
Within minutes other flames, followed by billowing
smoke, ignited throughout the city. Jill shook her
head in disbelief as she saw flames in the east,
imagining her caretaker's home being consumed by
the terrible orange fire.

Jill leaned against the trunk of a tree, and pulled
her arms around her chest, thankful that Salma
had given her the coat. Closing her eyes, she tried
to imagine where her caretaker would hide, what
means he would use to get there, forgetting, for a
moment, her new and terrible surroundings and
that when she stepped into the Forest she felt as
though she was leaving one terrible world behind
for another.

Chapter Two

When Jill opened her eyes the night had passed and the sun was shining across the meadow. Sunbeams met with the mist on the border of the forest and created patterns of rainbows in midair. It only took a few moments for Jill to reorient herself and remember where she was. She looked around, startled, as she recalled the hurried flight from the city the evening before, angry at herself for falling asleep so close to the edge of the meadow where she might be visible to the Watchmen.

The events of the last hours were still a blur in her mind. Jill tried to replay all the details, but couldn't make sense of them. It was like any other day. She had gone to school and through all her normal daily rituals of classes and study. As usual she waited in the park for her caretaker to meet her and accompany her for the rest of the long walk to his home. Unlike most other children, Jill was not allowed to walk on her own through Vendor. Nor was she allowed to cover her face like most other

citizens. Wherever she went in the city, her face
was exposed and uncovered, visible to all citizens, a
Daughter of Disgrace.

Jill waited for nearly an hour, enjoying her time
on a bench under a poplar tree, sketching in her
notebook as unseen birds chirped in the solitude of
the park. Her caretaker never arrived, the first time
since he became her caretaker that he was late, a
fact in itself unusual and alarming. When the curfew
alarm started to howl, Jill felt her first sensation of
anxiety.

Watchmen descended on the streets in their
yellow and green uniforms and started to usher
people to their homes. Men wearing dark red
masks with no features other than slits for the eyes
and mouths, frantically rushed along the street
murmuring to women covered with dark blue veils
a rumour: the Council had learned of another group
of citizens in Vendor harbouring escaped workers
from one of the labour camps outside the city. The
Council was going to search entire neighbourhoods
to find the culprits.

Jill could feel the tension of panicked citizens
on the streets as they ran to their houses while
the curfew siren wailed. In the last few weeks the
Council started aggressively interrogating and
imprisoning people when a story emerged that a
citizen of Vendor had contact with someone in the
Forest. The story unsettled people who for years
had been told by the Council that the Forest was no
longer inhabited, people who had learned to avoid
the Council's attention at all costs, especially to

raise no suspicions of disloyalty to the body. The contrary report about life in the Forest raised doubts about the Council's reliability. Doubts, if discovered by the Council, would lead to strict punishment, like banishment to the labour camps.

Upon hearing the rumour from where she sat inside the school park, Jill started to panic: how would she get to her foster home? Her caretaker was nowhere to be seen, and the Council enforced the strict law with a harsh public caning for any Shameface, a Daughter or Son of Disgrace, young or old, who was found alone on the street, not accompanied by a caretaker.

Jill felt sick to her stomach when she remembered the Watchman's words, they startled her: "Daughter of Disgrace, what are you doing out here alone? You are ordered to your home!" He wore a green uniform, but the mask on his face was orange, a junior officer.

"Sir," Jill replied nervously, almost unable to find her voice, "my caretaker has not arrived, I have been waiting for him for hours."

"Is your caretaker always so careless? Perhaps I should report him to the Council."

"No sir, he has never been late."

"Never? You have never waited long, perhaps until dark, then walked the streets alone?" The Watchman squinted at Jill through the slits in his mask. "What is his rank?"

"He's an Original, sir, he wears the white veil of the Council."

"An Original!" the guard whispered in surprise. He coughed, looked over his shoulder, and pulled at his collar. "A Councilman as a caretaker? I've never heard of such a thing." The Watchman was quiet for some time. "There must be a reason; the Council is wise and good and all shall honour it." Then, abruptly, "His absence can only be explained by the pressing crisis the Council faces. He is busy at work on behalf of the city, defending it against the threat of –" the guard took a step toward Jill and yanked her to her feet by her arm, "people like your parents who no doubt abandoned you for foolish things and covered you with their shame."

"Where are you taking me?" Jill asked, alarmed as he dragged her beyond the school gate and out of the park.

"To your home, and quickly, you will tell me the way. You know you can't walk the streets on your own. Your caretaker has taught well that you are a reminder to the people of the shame of Vendor's past, a past full of superstition, of stories, black magic. What grade are you in, girl?"

Jill frowned and looked up at the Watchman.

"What grade are you in?" he repeated slowly, as though Jill had not understood.

"Five."

"Then you are young, of the youngest, perhaps one of the last in the Council's program. When you are old and die, maybe then Vendor will be purged of indignity, of all those former things." The officer spat on the ground. A trail of saliva dripped from the edge of his mask, Jill watched it stretch until it touched her arm just above where the Watchman gripped her.

The Watchman escorted Jill home at a fast pace, holding her by the arm firmly. They weaved through the city streets from the school toward an edge of town. When she got to the foster home her arm was sore, bruised.

"There you are," the Junior Watchman announced, pushing her onto the cement step. "I've spared you from a caning tonight, though I'm sure you deserve it for *something*. You will tell your caretaker, tell him Junior Watchman Spake has done this."

"Yes sir."

"Now I leave." The Watchman put his hand over his heart. "For the Council alone."

Jill put her hand to her heart and mumbled back, "For the Council alone," and the officer was off.

Jill quietly walked up the steps and through the door. Her caretaker had a small house, it was unassuming, like all the others on the street, tucked away in the old neighbourhood behind large trees. When visiting members of the Council dined with her caretaker, they often commented on its smallness. Most members of the Council lived in mansions in the centre of the town or on streets where original but Shameless city members lived. The Council seemed to have no problem with old wealth, though it despised most other old things.

"Daughter, where have you been?" a worried voice met her as she entered the house. It was

Salma, the old servant who kept the caretaker's house.

"Salma," Jill replied, "he didn't come. I waited in the park for hours until it was dark. An orange Watchmen brought me home."

Salma shuddered. "Those cruel, evil men."

Salma was old, wrinkled, and hunched. She walked with a limp, but her age and manner were deceiving. She was sharp and feisty, and unafraid to speak critically of the Council, even in front of Jill's caretaker. She was forbidden to wear a veil, but Jill guessed even if she was permitted, she would refuse to cover her face.

Salma watched over Jill ever since she was moved into the foster home. Jill's caretaker knew Salma before the Council came to power in Vendor, before enforced curfews, before the mines and the masks. *She is the best help available in the city. She might be disgraced, but she is unmatched in her skill with an iron, and a wash basin, and a skillet,* Jill had heard her caretaker say when he defended his decision to let a Shameface manage his household. But then the visiting Council member would sit down to eat, and all his or her reservations about Salma would be lost in the delicious enjoyment of her food.

Sometimes when they were alone, when it was safe to risk it, Salma whispered Jill old stories of different times and far off places, stories with magic in them. These were Jill's favourite moments, but they were very few.

"Child, I was sick with worry. I thought they'd found you. I thought they had finally figured it out and taken you away."

Jill scrunched her nose. "Who did you think found me?"

"Terrible, horrible men, men who have been searching for you for a very long time."

Jill stopped unbuttoning her coat and looked up at Salma.

"Jill, there is very little time. It is not my story to tell. Take off that jacket and put this on."

Salma reached into the closet and pulled out a red wool jacket that had shiny golden buttons. Jill's jaw dropped. Salma returned to the closet, found a white box, and pulled out a thick gold veil.

"And this."

"Salma, where did you get these things? You know only Town Daughters can wear the red coat and the golden veil, and I'm not one of them."

"Jill, put them on."

"But if I'm caught, they'll –"

"You can't let them catch you. They *will* not. He will protect you."

"Who?"

Salma stopped, winked at Jill, then finally relaxed and smiled. "He who guards us all."

"How will he protect me?"

"You'll walk into that understanding when the time is right. No more questions, child, there is no time."

"No time for what?"

"You must walk away from here, away from Vendor, and not return. Leave the house, you can't be seen with your caretaker. Take Derby Road until it connects with Centre Street. You will find a street in the North called Ashlea. Speak with no one, for Town Daughters do not speak. There is a home on Ashlea Street that belongs to a member of the Council. She is on our side."

Our side.

"You will recognize it by its red gate. Go there. It's on the edge of town. From there you will be told what to do."

*　　*　　*

Though the sun was out, Jill shivered. Dew from the leaves and grass where she had fallen asleep soaked her pants and shoes. Her jacket, however, kept the moisture away from her body and kept her quite warm all through the night. Jill looked at her surroundings. She had imagined the Forest a number of times, and now she stood inside of it. Mossy beards hung from the trunks of trees that stood like giants frozen in time, their branches extended like arms in every direction so high into the air that the sun's light at midday would be blocked below them. Although she was only a few steps into the Forest, Jill noticed it was unnaturally dark and cool.

Though darker than the sunlit meadow, the Forest was a colorful place, and Jill found its sounds and smells startling. It had a permanent smell of spring rain, a smell that reminded Jill of water and earth and freshness. The mist from the night before remained and not only bordered the tree line of the Forest, but curled and moved along the path and disappeared into the darkness and underbrush of the trees. When Jill looked down she could no longer see the path or her feet. Her red coat with its gold shining buttons was visible, but her pants and walking shoes disappeared into the thick mist. In the daytime, Jill did not feel uneasy about being in the Forest. If anything she felt compelled to stay and explore, an overwhelming feeling so different from the night before, one she noticed but could not explain.

Jill saw that the Forest had many different types of trees. Trees with needles and trees with leaves. She imagined how thick the Forest floor would be with leaves in the autumn when Nature pulled them to the ground preparing the earth for snow. There were trees with dark brown bark that looked hard and strong as metal, and there were trees with white coloured bark that peeled at her touch, like snakes shedding skin. All the leaves were green, but at certain times, out of the corner of her eye, they seemed to glisten gold, shine red in hue, glimmer like silver. When Jill saw such colour flash in the corner of eye she would quickly turn, and as she did, the colours disappeared.

Further into the Forest, she could hear the sound of water. Soon she discovered a stream curving its way between rolling banks. At the sound of the water, Jill realized how thirsty she was. She tried to calculate how many hours it had been since she had a drink of anything. She knelt down at the water and awkwardly scooped it into her hand and drank from her palm.

At the stream's edge, the mist evaporated and Jill noticed in its place small blue, white, and yellow flowers. Purple heather was scattered and growing all about. Great, thick mosses coloured green and orange grew over fallen trees and all along the stream's banks, forming what to Jill looked like giant but soft beds. She longed to run and throw herself onto them, but continued to walk along the path.

Jill found some wild raspberries growing along the path and stopped to snack on them. They were overripe. The red berries were easy to miss, well hidden under large green leaves. The berries stained Jill's fingertips and tongue; they were sweet, and revealed to Jill how hungry she was. Jill rummaged through her pockets in hopes of finding some left-over snacks from the ones Salma had scrounged up from her caretaker's cupboards the night before. Jill found nothing but a single stick of chewing gum in her left outside pocket. She popped it into her mouth and then pulled out the letter she was given at the house with the red gate, after her nervous walk through the city, unaccompanied and veiled.

She had not been stopped or hindered in her illegal walk to Ashlea Street, though every step she feared a Watchman or a citizen would confront her, pull off her veil and reveal her shame. The green-veiled woman, a member of the Council with a

large house, met her at the door. All the lights were
off in her home, and she ushered Jill through the
house to a back room where, to her surprise, her
caretaker was busy at a table piled with papers.
The caretaker was leafing through the piled papers,
selecting certain documents, and throwing them into
a burning fire. But he stopped his urgent work, came
to Jill's side, and for the first time since they had
met, leaned down and hugged her to his chest.

Jill had never seen her caretaker's face, but she
imagined that it was kind, that it was a strong and
gentle face, noble like his eyes. In that moment she
longed to see it, even for a moment, but she did not.
Before he spoke with her, before he told her to run
with all speed to the Forest, he handed her a letter
and told her to open it only when she was in the
safety of the trees. Then he kissed her on the cheek.

*If they catch you before you reach the Forest,
destroy the letter. It cannot fall into their hands.
If you do not make it to the Forest, Jill, more lives
than your own will be lost. They cannot know he
still has contact with people inside the city.*

*   *   *

Jill held a neat white envelope, sealed with a
thick, blue wax seal in her hands. The envelope
looked like it came from somewhere important.
There was no return address or stamp, but had her
proper address on the front, written in plain, neat
letters:

Jill Strong
14 Sunrise Lane
Vendor, T4P 1J5

Jill looked up at the green canopy of leaves
above her, so different from the wooden roof under
which she was given the letter the night before.
Her mind buzzed. She turned the envelope over
and studied the wax seal. Upon closer examination,
she saw that it was imprinted with the profile of a
horse's face. Jill picked a small twig off the path,
slipped it under the seal and broke it. When Jill
pulled the letter from the envelope, shivers rushed
up and down her spine.

Jill unfolded the letter and noticed that it was
dated 7 February. It was more than nine months old!
Jill read the crisp, cursive letters. From the look of
the handwriting, Jill guessed that the writer wrote
hurriedly. The letter read:

Dear Jill,

Peace! If you are reading this letter, then
I rejoice. You are alive and well and your
time to enter the Great Forest has come.
Your caretaker has been a trustworthy caretaker and has kept you from the terrible
influence of the Council. It is he who has
decided the timing upon which you were
entrusted with our correspondence.

Doubtless you have many questions and
fears. These questions I cannot now address,

though I know circumstances in Vendor are grim. I can only assure you that while you are in the Forest, you are safe.

Jill, you must find your way along the path to the Great Hall, the home in the Forest that is under my charge. It is of utmost importance that you come quickly and come alone. Do not delay. I write this letter in haste, for there is trouble in some of the other lands under my charge that are beyond Vendor and the Forest. I must leave soon, I cannot tarry much longer. And when I leave on this journey I will be gone for some time.

Be of good courage, Jill. It is no coincidence you were born into the Strong family and bear that name. You come from a family of strength. Do not fear entrance to the Forest. In a little while, we will meet, and I will no longer be a name without a face. I look forward to that day.

Until we meet, perhaps to know each other by different names,

The Keeper of the Great Forest

Jill ran her finger over the name again. *The Keeper of the Great Forest*. The name seemed vaguely familiar. She tried to remember if she had ever heard Salma tell a story about him, but the effort was like trying to remember details from a long ago dream of the night.

Jill often found that real life seemed less exciting than the things she could imagine. In fact real life often left her disappointed. As she stood in the Forest, holding the letter, something inside told her that everything was about to change. She couldn't say why she felt that way, it was just something she all of a sudden knew. The same way she knew there would be a surprise quiz awaiting her at school, or that her poem would be the selected the prize winner in the War Veteran's Poetry Contest before she even entered it in the competition. No one had told her these things, but by some odd chance, without trying to, she had thought them before they happened. And when they turned out to be true her heart beat a little faster, and she could only wonder if she had been touched by some invisible magic. As Jill walked the Forest's path toward the mysterious Great Hall, her heart beat with that feeling.

Eventually Jill came to a point where the path intersected with the stream and she could go no further. The stream widened where it met the path so that it was too wide for Jill to jump across. Jill went to the water's edge and saw that the water was rather deep. She could not simply walk through it and hope only to get her shoes wet. Jill looked about for a log or some other thing she could use as a bridge to cross the stream but could find nothing. She turned back to the stream to test just how deep it was, and when she did, she stopped motionless in her tracks. In front of Jill was a tall creature, two or three times her own height wearing a dark black robe. The creature's face was hidden under a black hood. Jill could see only gray and black shadows instead of a face, like she was peering into a cave. She might have screamed, if the creature did not speak first, before she was able to think.

"What are you doing in the Forest alone?" The creature tilted its head to the side. "I can tell from the look of your dress you come from Vendor. But Town Daughters are usually veiled, are they not?"

Jill put her hands to her face, her hands went cold. She had discarded the veil when she awoke, unaccustomed and uncomfortable with its heat and limited visibility.

"You know that citizens from Vendor are not supposed to be inside the Forest."

Jill stared blankly at the creature for a moment. It was taller than a Watchman and cloaked differently. It was frightening to look at, but its voice was calm, if not kind. Jill was frozen, but found her bearings and remembered the letter. She fumbled with the button that closed her inside jacket pocket and pulled out the letter.

"See, it's written to me."

Jill stared at the creature then held out her hand, offering the letter. Jill gasped when the creature pulled back its hood, took the letter from her, and started to read it for itself. The creature looked like a man, a very tall man, but had dark blue skin. Purple markings in patterns like a tattoo traced all along the bridge of the creature's nose, parted at its forehead, and covered the creature's bald head along each temple down its neck. How far the purple pattern went, Jill could only guess, the rest of its body was shrouded in black cloth. The creature's eyes were most astonishing; dark brown irises, darker than the bark of the trees in the forest, were surrounded not by white, but by gold. They were the most extraordinary eyes Jill had ever seen.

Realizing she had been staring at the creature for some time, Jill blushed and looked at the ground, muttering a "sorry." The creature slowly nodded its head and suppressed a smile. Then, it returned to the letter.

"Why didn't you say you know the Keeper," it said, folding the paper into the envelope and handing it back to Jill.

"I don't. At least we've never met," Jill replied. "But it sounds like he knows me," she added quickly, more to herself than to the creature.

"You come at a strange time, under strange circumstances. Town Daughters do not carry such things."

Jill looked at the ground again and mumbled, "I am not a Town Daughter. I'm a Daughter of Disgrace."

"Such a letter has not been seen in this forest for quite some time."

"Why not?" Jill asked.

"Because the Keeper is no longer here."

"Where is he?"

"No one knows," said the creature with a sigh. "But the Keeper of the Forest is mysterious, has always been, and has many other lands under his care."

"I –" Jill stuttered with a look of bewilderment on her face. "Somehow I think I knew that."

"It says so here, in the letter."

"I know," Jill said, "but that's not what I mean. Suddenly I have a faint memory of this forest, like I've been here before. A memory of stories –"

"From who?"

Jill squinted her eyes and looked at the creature, trying to think, and after thinking, trying to decide whether she should tell him. As she looked at it, the creature exhaled loudly from his nostrils, let go of the envelope, and took a step back.

"Some from my caretaker's house in Vendor, and," Jill hesitated. "And, from my mother!" Jill breathed deeply. "My mother told me the stories when I was a little girl. They are the first stories I can remember. She had a –"

Jill stopped and looked away from the creature. A tear swelled in her eye. "She had a book full of them," Jill said, looking beyond the creature, far off into the woods across the stream.

"A book? What kind? Describe it to me, what did it look like?" the creature said hurriedly.

"It was big and heavy and old with pictures. Maybe that's where I've seen this forest. Oh, I can't remember. The Council, Vendor, since I've lived there I've forgotten so many things. It's like my memory of people, of places from before have been, have been erased. I've forgotten faces, names. But the book. The book is much older than this road, or the forest and its trees. I remember that. It was sealed shut with a lock that can only be opened with one key. A key that cannot be found."

Upon hearing Jill's explanation, the creature bowed to one knee and put its hand over its heart.

"Dear child, speak no further, for I have heard the story of your mother and also of the key. What was done to your mother was evil. But child, you need to remember those stories. They are as real as anything you can feel or touch. They are truer than all these things," the creature said, pointing to the trees around them, "and should not be forgotten."

"It's been so long since I heard them," Jill confessed, "I can hardly remember them at all."

"They are a part of you. They will be told again."

Jill smiled, and quickly brushed away the tear.

"Well," Jill said, clearing her throat, "I need to go to the Great Hall. Only, I don't know how to get there. The path I was told to follow runs into this stream, and it looks too wide and deep for me to cross alone."

"If you will, I can lead you down the path, for I am one of the caretakers of his Forest, and know the path well."

"Thank you, but I was asked to walk the path alone."

"I understand," said the creature, almost sadly. "Once you follow the stream, continue to follow the path, soon you will come to the house under the Keeper's care."

With that, the creature bowed once more then pulled the hood over its head. Once again Jill looked into the dark cave it created over the creature's face. Jill was about to ask him how he would help her cross the stream when she realized the Forest was completely silent. All the forest noises she had become used to – birds high in the trees, squirrels crawling about here and there, even the sound of the stream itself – were muted. Jill looked about and was shocked to realize that nothing in the Forest moved. There was no more breeze. The stream itself ceased to flow. A bird flying overhead froze in the air in mid-flight. Jill looked at the creature and it merely gestured with a move of its hand for Jill to cross the river.

Jill gave the creature a questioning look, and slowly walked to the water's edge. She crouched down and timidly touched her hand against the water. It was hard and solid as ice. Jill pulled her hand back in surprise. She looked back at the creature and smiled bashfully. The creature merely gestured again for her to cross. So, Jill slowly took a step onto the surface of the water, half fearing she might fall through, half disbelieving what she was about to do. When she put her weight on her foot she was relieved and amazed to see that she was standing on the stream. It was hard as ice, but still looked like liquid, only stopped or paused in time. Jill took a few more quick steps. The water was not slippery either. Jill made it to the other side of the stream and let out a whoop of laughter.

When she turned to thank the creature, it was gone. Jill looked back across a flowing stream and saw nothing but a streambed. The breeze softly blew hair across her face. The bird, moments earlier stuck in mid air, flew up and perched on the branch of a nearby tree.

Chapter Three

After crossing the stream, Jill continued down the path. As she walked, she thought over her conversation with the magnificent creature and the magic he used to cause the Forest to stand still in time. Jill could hardly believe the events that had just taken place. The thought of it made her giggle in astonishment. Jill was also surprised to hear that the Keeper had not been seen in the Forest for some time. She wondered what to do. What if he wasn't there? Where would she go? What would she do? Her caretaker had disappeared and it was not safe to go back to Vendor.

Jill felt anxious. All of a sudden she found herself alone in a strange new place with no plan, and she was at the mercy of someone who may or may not be around to help her. If Jill felt anxious, she had to admit to herself that she was also a little excited. She was like a vagabond: alone, on the road, totally vulnerable, but also very free. She concluded that the only thing to do was to walk to the Great Hall and see if anyone was home.

Jill followed the path until she entered a clearing. The dirt path that led her through the foliage ended when she stepped beyond the trees and connected to a walkway made up of flat, round stones, each one about the size of Jill's hand. The stone path brought Jill through a beautiful garden and up to a gate. Above the gate was a tall white arch covered with ivy. Behind the gate was a yard surrounding a very large house that Jill could only describe as *majestic*.

The gate was left open, pushed inward toward the house, and Jill walked through it to the porch. The stone path curved its way toward the front steps of the house, forming what to Jill looked like a very elongated S shape. Midway along the path were two stone pillars that rose nearly ten metres above the ground. Vines and moss covered the pillars. Jill stood in between them and stuck out her arms. If she stretched as hard and as far as she could, she could nearly touch each pillar at the same time.

From where Jill stood outside, the house looked old, impressive, lived in. The grass in the yard was short, flowers in pots were colourful and alive, no where could she see weeds. The entrance to the house was massive. Two solid oak doors loomed above Jill more than ten feet high. The door handles were bronze, shaped like the heads of valiant stallions, and were so brightly polished they glimmered like fire. Jill was astonished by the doorknobs, and leaned down to look at them more closely.

Each doorknob was a single sculpted bronze piece, which curved upward from the oak door so that it appeared as if horses were tossing their head from the ground in an upward arch towards the sky. The sharp, rigid equine jaws jutted out toward the porch, and the beasts' nostrils were flared up at the porch's awning. So real did they seem, Jill could almost hear hot breath leaving the horses' mouths as they neighed wildly. A single ruby was set deeply into each bronze face and shaped in the form of an eye. The ruby caught and reflected the light of he sun, which made the horses look alive. The horses faced each other, both heads tossed upward, as though charging in battle. Their beautifully textured manes were thick, and formed the handle which any soul, brave or foolish enough to tame such wild beasts, might grab hold of to enter the house.

Jill smiled at the horses, and touched the right door handle in awe, half expecting to feel the power of the horse's strength. Without meaning to, Jill pushed the door open with one light, reverent touch. Jill stepped back in surprise as the door creaked open. The room inside was enormous and rather dark. It was separated into two sitting areas by a very large staircase. Jill slowly took a step inside.

"Hello? Is anyone here?"

There was no response.

"It's Jill. Jill Strong? I've come to –"

Jill was interrupted by the sound of a loud *whoosh!* A fire ignited in the huge stone fireplace at the end of the room along the western wall. The rush of air from the fire created a draft in the room that pulled at Jill's hair and blew loose papers throughout the room from where they rested on end tables and bookshelves. A wave of air pulled Jill's body toward the fireplace and behind her the door shut loudly. Startled, Jill looked over her shoulder at the door, regaining her composure she called out again. She waited for a few moments, but no one responded. Jill looked around the room. *I'll just find a seat and wait*, she thought to herself, deciding the Keeper or whoever was watching the house had gone out for a few minutes or was busy in some back room.

Jill moved to a couch near to the roaring fireplace and sat down. Beside the couch was a small table with a vase that had two yellow flowers in it. Leaning against the vase was an envelope similar to the one her caretaker had given to her. Jill stood up and walked to the table. On the envelope, once again in neat letters, was her name, *Jill Strong*. Jill turned the letter over. On the back of the envelope was the same blue seal of wax. Jill looked to the door then back at the table. The emblem on the seal, which earlier in the day she had hardly paid any attention to was the same beautiful design as the sculptured bronze doorknobs. A letter opener rested on the table beside the envelope. Jill picked it up and in one swift slice broke open the seal. As she pulled out the letter, shivers once again tingled up and down her spine. She read the letter out loud.

37

Dearest Jill,

    The trip I spoke of beyond the Forest
was much more urgent than even I expected.
I trust that you arrived soon after you
received my first letter, as I requested.
I regret not being able to welcome you
personally into the home entrusted to my
care, but I hope you will understand that I
could not delay any longer.
    You must have many questions. My
letter to you and my request may sound
mysterious, but, for reasons you will understand at a future time, it must be that way.
    What I can tell you at present, in print,
is that your dear Mother once received a
similar letter with a similar request. She was
a trustworthy woman in every respect and
that good quality has been passed on to you.
Your mother kept for me a very important
book, a treasure beyond compare. The time
has come for one of the treasures belonging
to this house to be entrusted to you. All its
treasures are precious, far more precious
than a single life. Your mother gave her life
to protect the treasure given her. Be assured
Jill, for this reason she rests in peace.
    Since this home was built, many letters,
like the one you received, have been sent
to people in the city of Vendor. Few have
returned to the Forest or this house. There
are many reasons to be afraid, but none great

enough to refuse adventure. All who guard the treasures of this house will find adventure as they keep it in their care. Each treasure is unique. Some are ancient, some are new, all are of indescribable worth.

For you, child, a priceless near timeless treasure has been given to keep. Once it is in your possession consider it something very precious. Try to learn about it all that you can.

You must guard the treasure, it is more important than your own life. One day you will understand this. Until then you will have to trust my word, and remember the example of your Mother.

You will find the treasure somewhere in the Great Hall. For its safekeeping, it has been hidden from all others and from you. To find your treasure, here is a simple clue:

> *One not all*
> *and all but one*
> *your treasure can find*
> *Unlock destiny*
> *with the touch of a finger*
> *in the wink of an eye*
> *Come to the place*
> *where the stones cry*

When you have found the treasure, keep it with great care. Do not let it out of your sight; do not entrust it to any other person, for I put it under your watch and yours alone. Treasures there are many but servants of this house there are few. Beware. There are both man and creature that do not deserve your trust. To give the treasure to them would be dangerous. You cannot always trust appearances. Look for the mark of true servants of this house, but understand that sometimes you won't find it outwardly, but in the character of the heart.

I welcome you into my home. What is mine is yours; you are welcome into every room, you can read any book. Only treat all things as valuable possessions. Above all, protect what has been entrusted to you.

Most sincerely,

The Keeper of the Great Forest

Jill rested her arms at her sides. She sat back down on the couch and skimmed over the letter again. She felt faint with hunger and tired. She looked around the room: to the door, at the fire place, then stopped surveying the room when her eyes locked on a painting. The painting was of a family. A father, mother, and young daughter sat under a cherry tree that was in full bloom. The man in the painting wore a suit, and, with his back to Jill, he pointed to something in the sky. The woman in the picture wore a white summer dress and a summer hat, angled so that it covered her eyes. The woman leaned down to the ground, and it looked as though she was about to touch the toddler who sat on a picnic blanket. The toddler's face was the only face in the painting visible to Jill. The toddler, a little girl with light brown hair curled around her ears, looked blankly out of the painting. With one hand pointing in the same direction as the man, her other hand rested on her little knee.

Jill gazed at the picture for some time. Something about it was familiar, but she could not make the connection in her memory, a frustrating exercise as feeble as an effort to remove a skin of apple from between two molars with an awkward and tired tongue. Jill fell back against the couch.

"What have I gotten myself into?"

Chapter Four

The room was dark and cold, but Jill could not find her coat. The door slammed as a strong wind blew through the room. As the fire ignited, Jill heard the sound of a terrible, guttural laugh echo all around her. Startled, she dropped the letter that was in her hand, and watched as it was pulled in the direction of the fire. Jill reached for it but could not move. It felt like her feet were nailed to the floor. "No!" Jill shouted as the letter was pulled into the flames and slowly caught fire. When the letter was reduced to ash, the evil laughter stopped and the room was silent. Wind blew through the room once more and the fire disappeared as suddenly as it had come. Jill stood shivering and immobile. From the darkness of the fireplace she heard an almost inaudible whisper: *You will not succeed. I will stop you.*

Jill woke with a start. She was disoriented and afraid, relieved she had only been dreaming. The fire had burned down to its last embers, the room was mostly dark. She felt around the couch for the letter. It was not there! She dropped her feet to the ground and crouched over the armrest of the couch to look at the floor.

"Great, Jill, you've gone and lost the letter already! You fool, how do you expect to find and guard a treasure?"

"Now, child, don't be so hard on yourself," said a voice from somewhere in the room.

Startled, Jill let out a short shriek. She looked across the room, but saw no one. She surveyed the room, listening for sounds as her breathing slowed down. After a few moments when she heard nothing else, she said, out loud to herself, "Jill, you need some food in your stomach, you're starting to imagine things."

From the other side of the room Jill heard the sound of pleasant laughter. "I wouldn't be so sure. But it is true, hunger can do many things. Never go to sleep on an empty stomach, you're sure to have nightmares, or so they say. We better find you some food."

Once again Jill was startled. She stood up and stepped toward the fireplace where there was a little more light.

"Where are you? I hear you but cannot see you," Jill said. "Show yourself so I can know if I should fear you." Jill clenched her jaw and glanced about the room.

"Well said, child. Well said. Look over here, on the wall."

Jill looked onto the wall, in the direction of the voice.

"Beside the mirror."

Jill walked over to the mirror and looked into it, half expecting to see someone other then herself. All she saw was her own reflection. Jill tucked loose wisps of hair behind her ear.

"You've just about got it. I'm right here."

Jill looked beside the mirror at a painting of an old man holding a pipe. She squinted, and brought her face closer to the painting so she could see it more clearly in the low light. Her nose almost touched the canvas.

"Now there, not so close, an old man still needs his personal space, you know."

At that, a puff of smoke curled out of the painting. Jill coughed and stepped back, waving her hand in front of her face.

"What is this?" she asked.

"Did your caretaker not tell you anything about the place?" the voice asked through the cloud of smoke. "He was always so good at keeping secrets. Step back a little more, please, and I will show you."

Jill took a few steps backwards. As she did her stomach suddenly felt queasy. Her head felt light and swirly and little black dots formed all over her field of vision – the same sensation she had when she jumped out of bed too quickly in the morning. Jill put her hands on her knees to steady herself from falling. After a few moments, when she stood back up, an old man stood in front of her.

Jill stood, staring at him in amazement.

"Did you just –" Jill said and pointed at the painting.

The man winked at her then bent over and coughed. He dusted himself off and stood in front of Jill, then extended his hand. Jill accepted it, all the while staring in amazement at the old man.

"Pleased to meet you. You're much larger than I remember. It's been a long time.

You still have your mother's eyes. I'm Mr. Kay, but you can call me Gilbert if you like, for that is my Christian name. And you must be Jill."

Jill realized she had been staring, mouth gaping, for some time.

"Sorry," she said, it's just that, I –"

"You thought you were alone."

"I thought I was alone. What are you?"

"I already told you. I'm Mr. Kay and I'm pleased to meet you," he said, extending his hand, which Jill took again. "And you can call me Gilbert if you like."

"Are you – are you, real?" Jill asked hesitantly.

The old man laughed, a deep belly laugh. While he did, the pipe which he had not removed from his mouth since he started speaking, coughed out more smoke.

"Alive and well. Possibly more real than anyone you've ever met. Of course, when you meet my master, or the Keeper as you might know him, you'll have the same questions all over again. But he's able to answer the question definitively, once for all, as they say."

"But, how did you –"

45

"How did I do that? You'll learn, but not yet. What you'll discover is that things are often more real then they seem, especially in this house. There are many rooms and many doorways here that lead to other places."

"The other paintings?"

"Paintings and," the old man paused.

"And what?"

"Let's not get ahead of ourselves. One thing at a time. You said you were hungry?"

"I said that because I thought I was going crazy."

"A full stomach is a happy stomach, as they say. Come, let me show you my favorite room in the house: the kitchen."

The old man extended his arm in a sweeping gesture and bowed. Jill started to walk in the direction he pointed. "Can you — can you do that with the other paintings in the room?" Jill asked, curious as to the extent of his magic.

"Some of them."

"Only some?" She asked.

"Yes, only some. Don't look so disappointed. And some in other rooms as well.

I will move to the others when I am ready."

"When will that be?"

"Time – if you can call it that – time will tell."

*   *   *

Mr. Kay would have no other questions until Jill sat down to eat. When she finally relented, she was happy she did. The food was warm, filling, and good. Without noticing, the questions only moments earlier that were so urgent, drifted to the back of her mind. The room was quiet except for the old man's occasional sighs of delight. By the looks of it, he enjoyed his food far more than Jill could if she tried.

"Are you sure you'll have no wine?" he asked her, whimsically. "I picked the grapes myself, have been looking forward to opening this bottle for years. Today seemed as good a day as any. Have a glass."

Jill lifted her glass of milk into the air and smiled politely. "Thank you, but milk is good enough for me."

"Ah young one, you have so much to learn. The finer tastes of the palate among them, to be sure. But it's better we not rush things. It's good to wait until things are ready, or so they say. A good wine takes good time."

The old man was fat. The only thing bigger than his smile and the look of mischief in his eye, was his belly, which burst out like a great boulder from his waist. He wore thick glasses that made his eyes look bigger than they really were, and he had wild white hair on the temples of his balded head which pointed out in all directions. He wore a brown wool suit but unbuttoned his top button and loosened his tie when he sat down to eat.

Once he finished his ample meal, Jill waited what seemed like forever as the old man stared at his glass, humming under his breath. When she put her empty milk glass back on the table, she did it with a thump, but that didn't wake the man from his happy dream. When she pushed her chair away from the table so that it scraped across the wooden floor, the old man didn't notice. Finally, Jill put her hand to her mouth and cleared her throat twice.

"Oh," said Mr. Kay. "Oh, right. Where were we?"

"Well, I had some questions I wanted to ask you."

"Yes, you did." The old man cleaned his top teeth and gums with his tongue.

"Well, they can wait." The man reached into his pocket and pulled out an envelope. Jill leaned into the table with a look of recognition.

"Hey, that's mine!"

"Easy does it, easy does it. No need to worry. I was just holding on to it for you.

Don't want a letter like this to fall into the wrong hands now do we?"

"Did you read it?"

"Child! What do you think I am, a thief? I didn't read it, and I will not read it.

Letters like this are to be read only by those to whom they are given, and those whom the letter carrier chooses to share them with." Mr. Kay hesitated, looking a bit flustered. "I've been a good friend of your family for over three generations, and I would expect to be treated as such from you, young lady."

Jill blushed in embarrassment when she realized how silly her outburst was.

"I'm sorry," Jill said, truly meaning it. "When I woke and couldn't find it I was worried. I'm glad to see it safely in the hands of a trusted family friend. Thank you."

The old man slowly handed the letter back to Jill. His face was suddenly stern. He pulled out his pipe and lit it. He puffed out his cheeks and let out a few clouds of smoke.

"I don't need to read the letter, Jill. I've seen many like it leave and return to this house. You'll find what you seek upstairs. That is all I know and that is all I can say. It is yours to guard and to keep, that is, until he takes it back for himself." Mr. Kay pulled the pipe from his lips and pointed it at the letter. "Take seriously the words of that letter. Those things you long to know, the questions you have forming on your tongue, you will discover them as you go. Don't be afraid to go slow. But, you will find your own pace. I must go now. Perhaps I'll see you again."

"So soon? We just met."

"You're fed. Soon you will be tired. Sleep wherever and in whatever room that seems good to you. Make yourself comfortable." Mr. Kay smiled, suddenly warm again. "Make yourself at home."

"When will I see you again?"

"Whenever I am told. Time, if you can call it that, will tell. Time will tell."

The old man looked to a far off place, beyond Jill, beyond the kitchen walls. For awhile she experienced near total silence and was lost to the rhythm of her own breathing.

"Well, that's that," he said. The man winked at Jill and smiled. "I'm off."

And with that he turned. Before Jill could speak, he pointed to a picture beside the fridge, ran with a speed that Jill didn't think he was capable of, and jumped toward the wall. For Jill, it felt as if the whole room bent and spun. The tables and chairs moved about like rubber. Her eyes watered and she felt nauseous. Then, just as quickly as the sensation began and her knees went wobbly, the room was normal again. The table was a wooden table; the fridge was a metal fridge. But the old man was gone.

In the distance, as if very far away, Jill heard the old man hoot and holler. His laughter made her giggle out loud until she realized she was alone in the room.

Jill walked up to the picture and slowly, carefully touched it with her hand. She was almost surprised when her finger was stopped by the glass covering the photograph; she half expected her arm to disappear like the old man did, right into the picture. At different angles, she could see her own reflection in the glass or the smudge of her fingerprint where she touched it. She shook her head then frowned.

"I hope I see you again, Mr. Kay."

Chapter Five

After Mr. Kay disappeared into the wall, Jill finished her milk and did the dishes, which was rather easy, since the old man had polished off the food so that they were virtually spotless, and only needed a rinse. Jill felt alone and sad in the quiet, newly aware how much she enjoyed the funny old man's company. She hardly knew him or anything about him, but learning that he was a good friend of her family made him somehow feel like he was family himself. It was a comfort to know her parents had a close friend. Mr. Kay gave her hope that she would learn more about her parents and that someday, some of the many questions she had might be answered.

When she finished the dishes, Jill stepped to the large glass door at the back of the kitchen. It opened onto a porch which overlooked a long yard where a small stream snaked its way from the woods on the western side of the property through grass and wild flowers, only to return once again into woods that bordered the field to the north. On the eastern side of the yard, a field much larger than the yard bordered a fence. Large wooden fence posts connected together by three lengths of barbed wire were evenly spaced along the field.

Jill stood at the door and looked out the window for some time, waiting to get a glimpse of what she might see in the field. The field went far eastward and rose into a slight hill beyond which she could see nothing else but sky. Yet no animal or creature came into view the whole time she stood at the glass door. It was only when the sun started to disappear behind the tops of the trees that she turned from the glass. She reached her hand into her pocket and pulled out the letter Mr. Kay had returned to her.

"Well, Jill," she said outloud to herself, "no sense in waiting any longer, better go find this treasure and keep it like the Keeper has asked you to. You can't stand here and think about horses forever."

Jill skimmed over the letter again and read the clue one more time:

> *One not all*
> *and all but one*
> *your treasure can find*
> *Unlock destiny*
> *with the touch of a finger*
> *and the wink of an eye*
> *Come to the place*
> *where the stones cry*

Jill entered the hallway that connected the kitchen to the front of the house. It was then she realized how dark it was getting and how unfamiliar she was with the house.

"Silly girl, you've been off in your own little dream world, and now you've got a dark house to explore, all on your own. You've got to start paying more attention to the obvious." Jill stopped in her tracks and laughed, catching herself repeating the words Ms. Steinback, her schoolteacher, said to her more often than she liked to admit. "And to top it all off, you're starting to sound like that old grump, Ms. Steinback.

Jill walked with her hand against the wall and stopped when she entered the front room. Nowhere on the wall could she find a switch to turn on a light. She reached the end of the hall and found herself in the room where she had discovered the second letter after she arrived at the Great Hall. The fire was completely extinguished, and the curtains on every wall, except beside the front door, were shut. Jill started to feel uneasy.

She walked over to the mirror, looked at herself and frowned. Then she looked up at the painting that old Mr. Kay had emerged from earlier in the afternoon. She was not surprised but was a little perplexed to discover that the painting was no longer the portrait of an old man smoking a pipe. It had completely changed. In his place was the picture of a large elephant walking on a tight-rope that spanned a great canyon. The elephant was being led by a man wearing a white turban.

Jill turned quickly to look at the other wall, curious to see if the other painting she had examined earlier had changed too. To her relief, the painting of the man, woman, and the young child still hung in its thick frame. The man was still pointing at something in the distance, the woman was bending down to touch her child, and the young girl with that curious expression on her face was looking right at Jill.

"Mr. Kay, I wish you were still here to help me find my way through this house, or at least help me find a light switch or two."

A large staircase fell from the second story of the house and descended to the main floor like a waterfall. The stairs were rounded in the front and curved back into the staircase at the edges. Two thick, dark wood banisters carved a pathway between which Jill could walk. As Jill stepped toward the stairs, the banisters remided her of the shape a large cello.

Jill put her hand on one of the banisters. It was cold to the touch. In daylight she imagined it would virtually shine, that's how smooth and polished it felt. The moment she stepped onto the first stair, both banisters suddenly glowed white, then one by one, each stair lit up with light. When Jill looked at her hand on the railing, it glowed bright orange-red, the same colour her skin turned when she pressed a flashlight into her fingertips or against her cheek in the dark.

When she looked more closely at it, she saw the staircase and banister had somehow been trans-

formed into the purest, whitest ivory. Jill gasped
at the beautiful pattern carved into the stairs and
banister. Everywhere she looked there were engrav-
ings of birds and flowers and words from a language
she could not read. And, in the middle of each stair,
set in the ivory, was a beautiful golden tree with
large branches and many leaves. Words in the same
script curled up the tree and around its branches.

Jill turned to the painting where the old man
used to be and smiled, convinced that somehow
Mr. Kay heard her request for light. She said "thank
you" then started walking up the stairs. If she had
looked at the painting a moment or two longer, she
might have seen the elephant flap its ears then reach
forward and lift the white turban off the man's head
with its trunk.

The stairway opened into a small sitting area
with couches, end tables and other sitting room
things. There were paintings everywhere, and
another fireplace, which was warmly burning in
a stone hearth. The sitting area split off into three
hallways, one that ran away from the staircase
toward the back of the house, and two that went
opposite directions toward the eastern and western
walls of the house. At the top of the stairs, Jill's
attention was immediately drawn to a green light
moving in one of the closest rooms. When she
stepped away from the stairs toward it, the staircase
went dark again, which also made the room grow
dim. Jill smiled and shook her head. "Where am I?"

Jill walked toward the room, curious to see
what was inside. In the dimmed light, she could

see that the green light scrolled from left to right. Jill tilted her head to the side and smirked. "Is that what I think it is? I was expecting something, well, magical," she said with a chuckle.

When she entered the room, she discovered that she had guessed correctly. The green light scrolling from side to side was the welcome message of a CD player. The rest of the room was dark. Jill bent over to read the small green letters:

Welcome to the Music Room of the Great Hall. Hear you are loved; Hear you are trea-sured; Hear and let great music be heard.

"Hmmm," Jill breathed. She reached forward and touched a button that had a little green triangle pointing like an arrow to the right. If Jill knew what was to happen next, she might have hesitated to press PLAY. But Jill had never been into the Music Room of the Great Hall before. When she pressed the button, an electric shock jolted from her fingertip through her entire body, and before she could shout, "What Have I Done!" she was thrown into the air, blown back by the speakers the way she blew tufts of dandelion seed into the air.

It was the impact from the bass woofer that threw Jill into the air, and when the air from the speakers hit her, her eyes closed shut. Jill kept them shut because she didn't want to watch herself hit the ground. The bass kept booming, so loud and deaf-ening that she could hear nothing else. The sound pounded through her body and thumped against her heart the same way the drum of a marching band had pounded through her during an outdoor parade in Vendor. But in the Music Room of the Great Hall, it felt like the marching band marched inside her body, through every organ and part.

It took Jill a few moments to realize she felt no impact of the fall at all. She slowly opened her eyes, so she could survey the damage done to her body. When she opened her eyes she screamed a loud, terrible scream of terror, which she could not hear over the noise of the music. The floor had fallen away, and was replaced by grass and trees that were very far below her. She was suspended above them, high in the air! All about her was the blue colour of sky and the whiteness of whisping clouds. Jill screamed again.

But, once she realized she was not going to fall, and that somehow gravity did not try to pull her to the ground, Jill took a deep breath. She moved her hand to her face to brush the hair that had fallen in her eyes, and as she did, she moved across the sky. Jill let out a short shout, and then a quiet laugh that grew louder and louder. She noticed that the boom of the bass once so loud and rapid had quieted and slowed down. She put her hand to her heart to feel its pace, and as she did, twirled in the air. When she felt her heart beat it was slower, calmer, in exact rhythm with the boom of the bass sound she heard.

Soon Jill discovered that moving in the air was not much unlike swimming in water, only she could breathe better and move more gracefully in the sky. For a long time she threw herself at the clouds and

spun in the air like the swallows she watched from
her window at school, no longer having to imagine
the birds' happiness at the sensation of flight.
She turned and dove and climbed, all the while
whooping and shouting out loud. Each time she did,
if she had been listening carefully (her ears at the
time were not trained yet to distinguish the slighter
nuances of music) she might have heard the sound
of crashing cymbals, the high notes of trumpets, or
the roll of the tympany whenever she shouted. Then
she plunged deeper and deeper toward the ground.
As she descended, pulling herself downward to the
trees and grass, so did the notes of music down the
musical scale. It was only then that she realized her
movements in the air made different movements in
the music. She also realized that she was outside
the house, above the yard and field and the trees
she had looked out upon earlier that day, after her
supper with Mr. Kay.

Jill made a dive for the field and stopped short
of the fence. She grabbed onto a post and pulled
herself toward it. She puffed out air like a helium
balloon and lightly, as a feather, touched the ground.
The moment she did, she heard the sweet spirited
sound of a horse's neigh. When she looked across
the fence to the rise in the field, over the hill she
saw a beautiful black horse canter towards her. It
was darker than ebony with a flowing mane. Jill
held out her hand and the horse approached her. Hot
breath shot out its nostrils against the palm of her
hand. The horse had a diamond-shaped star, white
as the ivory staircase, and no larger than Jill's hand,

in the middle of its forehead. Jill leaned over the
fence and pushed her forehead against the horse's,
then closed her eyes. She let out a laugh of delight.
When she opened her eyes the horse stepped back,
tossed its head in the air and stomped its foot
against the ground, all in time with the music.

The horse stepped back toward Jill, and she
noticed that the white diamond on the animal's forehead had turned into a red square. She leaned her
cheek against the horse's cheek, and slowly slid her
hand toward its forehead. As she did, the horse tried
to pull away, but Jill grabbed it by the mane and
steadied the beast. With her left hand she quickly
touched the red spot on the horse's forehead.

Jill's stomach went queasy and she closed her
eyes. Her knees wobbled and her mouth went dry.
Everything was silent. Jill could only hear the
sound of her breathing. When she opened her eyes,
Jill let out a gasp. Her finger wasn't touching the
forehead of the horse anymore, but the red STOP
button on the CD player. Instead of a beautiful dark
horse face and deep brown horse eyes, Jill's cheek
rested agaisnt the cold black CD player. Green
text scrolled across the player's display where she
thought the horse's eyes should be. It read:

*Thank You for Playing Your Song; Your
Music Has Been Heard*

Jill pushed the EJECT button, curious to see
if there were any CD in the player or if by some
miracle or magic, and not because of her over active

imagination, she had really experienced her whole flight. The disc tray slid smoothly toward Jill, and sure enough, a CD, blue in colour, rested inside the tray. Jill stuck her index finger into the hole at the centre of the disc and lifted it out of the player. Jill spun the disc so the title of the CD was right side up. It said:

Jill Strong: The Flying Fields (A Collection of Songs).

Jill scrunched her face, puzzled. As she stood turning the CD around in her hand, the disc tray slid to a close. Jill looked back at the player when she heard the sound of hard plastic hitting the ground. At her feet was an empty CD case. Jill bent over to pick it up. An album cover was inserted behind the plastic of the casing. On it was a picture of girl in a red coat, hair streaming across her face, arms extended towards the sky. Below the picture in white letters was *The Flying Fields* followed underneath by her full name. Jill let out a slow whistle.

Jill looked around the Music Room. Since her music had stopped playing, the lights in the room, somehow, had been turned on. The room was small. There was soft brown paint on the walls. There were no chairs or couches or paintings. Only a small little table with the CD player on it sat in the middle of the room, and a metal music stand stood off in one of the corners. A shelf filled with CD's formed a continuous line on all four walls of the room. The shelf was about as high as Jill's chin, and she had to stand on her tiptoes to see the tops of the CD cases. Jill put her CD on the shelf where there was an empty space, then walked over to the music stand. On it was a white book. Jill picked it up and read the title:

The Music Room, A New User's Guide.

Jill flipped the book open to the first page and started to read. She turned and looked at the player when she read the first line. In bold print it said:

RULE # 1:

**THE FIRST RULE IS THE ONLY RULE:
DO NOT PRESS PLAY UNTIL YOU READ
THROUGH THE MANUAL.**

Jill blushed, then sat down on the floor. She decided she had a little reading to do.

Chapter Six

Jill left the Music Room, but promised herself she would go back and visit later. She was starting to feel tired after the events of the day, but was determined to do what she could to find the treasure before she went to sleep. So, she started to explore the upstairs. She walked down each hallway and quietly, cautiously opened the doors. Sometimes she would knock first to be polite, but, as she expected, met no one else in the house.

There were a dozen or so rooms upstairs along the east-west corridor, some large and some small like the Music Room. Rooms Jill determined to explore later were the Library, a massive room with overstuffed chairs, books on shelves along each wall standing more than two stories high with large ladders on rolling wheels, and a fireplace big enough for her to lie down in as she would have done, had there not been a large fire blazing in it at the time. The Games Room with it's board games, trivia, and puzzles. The Planetarium with it's glass

covered ceiling and telescopes, and the Theatre
Room which had a stage covered by dark purple
curtains from which hung thick golden tassels. The
names of each room were engraved deeply into little
wooden signs that were fitted against the oak finish
of each door. Jill found three beautiful bathrooms
with checkered floors and white free-standing tubs
that stood on brass feet. She did not enter any of the
rooms, but looked inside them from the doorway.
It took all her self-control not to enter each room to
explore; she forced herself just to look so she could
get a feel for the place, before she tried to solve the
clue left to her in the letter.

Jill saved the corridor, extended beyond the
stairway which led toward the back of the house,
for last. Something, some faint impression, told her
to wait to walk down that hall; somehow she knew
that it was down this hallway she would come upon
her treasure. When she finished exploring the other
hallways, she came back to the sitting room at the
top of the stairs and sat down. She warmed herself
by the fire and after a few minutes of rest and a few
more yawns, she stood up and started to make her
way slowly down the remaining hall.

The first room she came to was called The
Boot Room. Curious, Jill turned the door handle
and peered inside. As with many of the rooms, the
Boot Room was lined with shelves on every wall.
On these particular shelves was footwear of every-
kind. Shoes and boots for every possible activity
or occasion. Shoes for running and hiking, shoes
for dancing and walking, shoes for racing and

climbing. There were flippers for people to wear
in the sea. There were wide shoes that looked like
tennis racquets with funny straps for people to walk
on snow. There were boots with sharp metal blades
for people to skate on ice. Sandals for the beach.
Cleated boots for football. Soft looking slippers
with hardened toes for ballet. There were shoes for
children, for men, for women. Shoes, shoes, shoes.
Some places along the wall were empty, as though
people had come, found the right pair that fit and
run away with them. Jill had never been fond of
shoes like some girls who had too many pairs to
count, but there were some in the room she wanted
to keep for herself upon her first glance.

On the opposite side of the hallway, Jill stopped
in front of a door that said The Armoury. Perhaps
with more curiousity than with which she opened
The Boot Room door, Jill turned the handle. When
Jill looked around the room, she could not supress
her astonishment. The room was filled with shining
metal swords and shields, and battle-ready armor.
Jill had never seen anything like it before. She had
only read about weapons in books. She had never
touched or held a real sword. Jill stepped into the
room and walked along the walls. Above the racks
from which the swords hung were paintings of
noble men on horses, swords drawn and pointing
in the air. There were paintings of battlefields, with
kingly banners upon the heights blowing in the
wind.

Jill stopped in front of a small painting set in a
gold frame near the centre of the room. The painting

was of a young girl on a white horse, who did not look much older than Jill. The girl's hair was short, cut almost like a boy's. She wore no armour but for a silver breastplate that had a flower engraved in white gold. The girl held a sword by the flat of the blade which spread across both her hands. The sword looked about as long as the girl was tall. Her hands were raised in the air, the sword above her head, as a sunbeam broke through the grey clouds and reflected light off of the edge of her blade. Behind the girl, on horses, were hundreds of men, in full metal, swords and bows drawn, ready to fight.

As Jill stared at the painting, a tear formed in her eye. Jill noticed a caption on the gold frame of the painting as she wiped the tear from her cheek; four simple words in plain text:

Jean d'Arc, heroine.

Jill felt heat and courage swell in her heart, a sensation she did not try to conjure up or to understand. Underneath the painting was a metal blade, almost the size of Jill, like the one in the painting. Before she could think, Jill put out her hand to touch the blade, which hung from the wooden rack toward the floor. She gripped the hilt of the sword and thrust her arms upward to release the weapon from the rack. Soon the hilt was over her head, the end of the blade pointing to the floor at her shins. Jill could hear her heart pounding loudly in her ears, her body tingled with excitement.

Suddenly, however, she realized the sword was much too heavy for her to hold alone, and the adrenaline coursing through her body, which had helped Jill pull the sword off the rack, would not help her hold the blade over her head much longer. Jill leaned forward and tried to slowly set the sword back on its rack, but she leaned too far. Her knees buckled beneath her as the sword pulled her upper body toward the ground. Jill looked between her feet when she heard the sound of spliced wood, not unsimilar to the sharp, clear sound of wood being cut by an axe. The weight of the sword no longer pulled at her muscles. The hilt of the sword now stood midway between her waist and shoulder, a length of the blade had disappeared beyond the plane of the wooden floor.

Jill swallowed the lump in her throat when she realized how close the blade had come to slicing through her foot. She scolded herself before she stepped up to the sword and tried to pull it loose from the floor. It would not budge. Jill gave the sword a few more tugs, then gave up trying. She sat on the floor and wiped away the drops of sweat that had formed on her forehead.

Feeling sheepish, she stood back up once she caught her breath, and looked at the painting again. "Well Jean d'Arc, guess I'll have to come back later. I'll have to figure a way to get the sword out from the floor. Until then, keep an eye on it for me, OK? Whoever you are, you sure make an impression."

With that, Jill turned from the wall and walked back to the door and out of the room. There were only three other rooms in the hallway. The next door Jill came to was The Study. Convinced there could be nothing of interest and no treasure behind that door, she moved across the hall to a door that said *Private* in large letters. The words were written on a wooden sign that was different then all the other names of the rooms marking the other doors. Underneath the letters was an eyehole set in the wood so that a person on the other side of the door could check to see who waited outside of it in the hallway. Instantly curious as to what lay inside, Jill knocked twice. After what seemed like a few minutes, Jill, satisfied she had honoured the privacy of whoever might be inside the room, turned the knob and pushed against the door to open it. The doorknob would not turn. It was locked.

Frustrated, Jill pushed her ear against the door to test if she could hear any sound inside. She heard no sound at all.

"Well, Jill, you have two options, you can either kick the door down and see what's inside, or obey the sign on the door."

Jill briefly thought of running back to The Armoury and finding a small sword or battering ram, but was only half serious. As she turned away from the door, she decided to peer inside the eyehole and look in. She stood on her tip toes and pressed her cheek into the door, then, shut her left eye tightly like she had just bit into a lemon and opened her other eye really wide. Jill moved her eye back and forth. She couldn't see much at all. What she could see was fuzzy and distorted, like looking through a magnifying glass backwards, underwater, with very little light.

To Jill, it looked like there was some furniture against the walls, and candles burning in the centre of the room. Just as she was about to step away from the door, Jill thought she saw something move. A dark object in the corner? Before she focused her eye to the corner of the room where she saw the shadow move, her legs started to cramp and she had to return, flat-footed, to the floor. Jill realized she had been holding her breath the whole time she looked through the eye hole. After a few moments, Jill got back on her toes and looked through the eyehole.

When she peered through the glass hole, her breath stopped: she looked directly into a big, green eyeball! Jill fell back from the door and walked quickly toward the other rooms, keeping her eye on the door the whole time. After a while, when she had collected herself, Jill said out loud, rather weakly, "I'm sorry if I disturbed you. I was just curious to see if anyone else was in the house. I'm a visitor here. I thought I was alone."

Silence. Jill took a step toward the door and cleared her throat. "I said, I'm new here. I thought I was alone. My name is Jill. Hello?" Under her breath, she said, more as a question to herself, "Am I just imagining things?"

Jill stepped up to the door again, over her surprise. She knocked, but no one answered. She pressed her ear against the door, but heard nothing. Finally, she forced herself to look once more, through the eye hole. She peered through it for only a moment. In that brief glance, she noticed the candlelight in the middle of the room had been snuffed out. She saw only darkness: no moving shadows, no furniture, and to her relief, no eyeball. Only the hazy rounded view of a magnifying glass held backward underwater with no light.

Jill felt comforted to tell herself that nothing and no one was behind the door. She did a good job convincing herself she was just letting her imagination get the best of her, but could not shake, completely, the feeling that she was not alone in the house. The butterflies in her stomach and the beat of her heart told her otherwise.

Chapter Seven

There was only one more room in the hallway that Jill had not examined. It was at the end of the hall. Instead of a door, thick, flexible plastic strips hung from the top of the entryway to the floor. A sign above the arched entryway read: The Atrium. As Jill pushed through the plastic and stepped into the room, she could smell the sweet scent of summer flowers, hear the gurgling of fountains, and feel humid air condense against her skin. Across from the entryway was an enormous paneled wall of tinted glass that curved at the top towards her and connected with the ceiling. The Atrium overlooked the back yard of the house, and from the room, Jill could see the woods and the field behind the house. Jill thought it odd that the room was filled with what appeared to be warm sunlight, even though it was dark as night outside the house.

The Atrium was filled with all kinds of plants: green plants growing from the floor to the roof, vines that curled and crawled around lattice and brick, and plants that hung from pots dangling down from the roof. There were flowers of every colour; tomato and cucumber plants and other vegetables; small trees and shrubs that were trimmed into the shape of animals. The Atruim was the biggest room yet. There were ponds with many fish; Koi, and Cat and Goldfish. But some of the ponds were empty of water and fish. Throughout the entire room, which seemed much larger than any room that could fit in a house, were pathways lined with white stones. Small birds fluttered throughout The Atrium. Once or twice Jill ducked and pulled her hands to her head to keep from being hit by birds that swooped low where she walked. Everywhere Jill looked there were stone sculptures among the plants and flowers in the room.

After walking through the room, Jill realized that the paths were set in three circles. The smallest circle, at least three times as wide as Jill was tall, was centred in the middle of the room. The second circle was centred in the third and largest circular path which nearly touched the central point of each of the four walls. On each side of the circular paths was ample vegetation. The two outer circles were divided by pathways that went from the smallest circlular path, diagonally toward the outer walls. There were eight such paths in all. Jill imagined that, if she were able to fly to the ceiling and perch on a hanging flower pot like one of the birds swooping at her head, she would see the pathways making a pattern not very different from a dart board.

Jill picked a ripe, red tomato from a tomato plant. She rubbed it against her shirt then bit into it like she was biting into an apple. The tomato was sweet and juicy, the most delicious tomato she had ever eaten. Jill was very hungry after all her exploring through the house, thirsty as well. She was tempted to lean over one of the fish ponds and lap up water like a farm animal, but thought it better not to. She was happy she didn't when she found a drinking fountain tucked away behind a tall mango tree.

Jill noticed something she had not realized at first. None of the statues had faces. They were all sculpted from greyish stone that Jill guessed was marble. The statues were carved out of the stone into men, women, cherubs, and animals, whose bodies were strong and athletic. The muscles and clothing looked like real muscles and clothes. Ocassionally, Jill looked over her shoulder, half expecting the statues to move and start laughing at her, revealing, after all this time, they were real people pretending to be statues, like the visiting street performers Jill had seen earlier in her life, before the Council had banned such things in Vendor.

The statues were beautiful but eerie. The women had long flowing robes and beautiful hair that looked like it blew lightly in a breeze, but instead of faces they had slabs of flat gray stone. The men looked active and strong as though they resisted some great invisible power that pushed against their muscled bodies. But they had no faces either. To Jill it looked like someone had pulled a thick marble visor over their heads.

Jill walked around the outer circle then along every diagonal path and wouldn't allow herself to go to the central circle until she had walked every other path in the room. When Jill had walked each path in one continuous circuit, she arrived at the central and smallest circular path. It made a circle around the largest fish pond in The Atrium. At the bottom of the pond, under the lilly pads and a lone fish that slowly swam about, Jill noticed some coins.

"It's a wishing pond," Jill excalimed, then rummaged through her pockets to find a coin. She had none, not even a penny.

Standing beside the pond was the largest, most beautiful statue among all the others in the room. The stone was different in texture and colour than all the other statues. It was light brown, porous to the touch, the way Jill had heard coral was in ocean reefs.

Light blue flowers grew all about the base of the sculpture and made the statue look as though it floated on a soft cloud. Jill had never studied sculpture, so she didn't know that the name for the way the statue stood was *Contrapposto*, meaning one leg was fully extended, while the other was slightly bent at the knee, so that the weight and form of the statue's upper body leaned toward the straightened leg.

The statue's right arm crossed over its chest covering the place where, if the statue was a real person, the heart would be. The left arm was extended away from the statue, palm outward. The statue's left index finger stretched up toward the roof, pointing at something in the air, like it was about to touch something. From its shoulders portruded great wings like the wings of an eagle. If they were stretched out into their full wingspan, Jill guessed the ends of the wings would extend beyond the white stones of the first circular path in the middle of the room. Instead, the wings rested neatly behind the statue, extending above the head then falling down its back like two massive capes. It looked as if, at any moment, the statue might soar into flight.

Jill stared at the statue in awe and hesitated to move, so real and awesome did it look. The statue's head looked like a round orb covered in clear, shining glass. Jill could see her own reflection in the statue's faceless face; a reflection that looked small and insignificant. She took a step closer to the statue and examined the face more closely. Behind what looked like glass, Jill could see movement. At first Jill thought it might be a shadow or her reflection. But after standing completely still and holding her breath for what seemed like minutes, Jill saw the movement again. A small drop of water formed then suddenly disappeared.

Jill discovered that if she wasn't looking closely at the face, or if she blinked, she would miss the movement entirely. Every once in awhile, in inter-vals about as long as she could hold her breath before gasping for air again, a small drop of water would appear on the glass-like face about where, if it had one, the statues left eye would be. Then, the water would fall onto the arm that was pulled across the statue's chest. The droplets of water collected in a pool at the elbow until the water overflowed and spilled into the wishing pond. Jill realized that the glass-like appearance of the statues 'face' was actually glass over water. She guessed that a pipe somehow connected the pool to the statue so that the water could circulate, probably, she thought, as a way to give the fish more oxygen.

Come to the place
where the stones cry

Jill felt a sudden rush of energy as she recalled the end of the clue she had been given earlier. "The place where the stones cry," she whispered out loud. "Could this be it?"

Excited, Jill looked more closely at the statue, put her hand against the torso, and slowly walked around it looking at every part. Jill pulled out her letter. *"One not all and all but one your treasure can find.* Come on treasure, you've got to be here somewhere. How can I find you? *Unlock destiny.* Unlock your destiny, eh? How? How do I unlock my destiny? It sounds so easy: *with the touch of a finger and the wink of an eye."*

Jill circled the entire statue, examining it with the interest of an inspector at a crime scene. She pulled at the statue's wings, put her finger in its belly button. She jumped in the air and tapped the glass-like face with her knuckles. She crouched down and crawled through the flowers at the statue's feet to look for a secret or hidden button. She found nothing.

"Well, maybe you got the clue all wrong. Maybe it's just a coincidence that water drips from the statue, and so what really is a coincidence you think is a real find. So much for paying attention to detail Ms. Steinback," Jill said sarcastically.

Jill sighed loudly and blew the hair away from her face. "Well, Mr. Statue, it was nice meeting you. Sorry to disturb you, I obviously have the wrong person. Take care of yourself."

As Jill moved to explore elsewhere, she waved goodbye, lifting her hand to the same height that the statue's hand was extended in the air. As she turned, out of the corner of her eye, she saw the finger glow bright orange. Jill did a doubletake. When she looked at the hand again, it was the same colour as the rest of the stone. Jill could start to hear Ms. Steinback's voice in her head scold her for an overactive imagination. Jill ignored the voice and lifted her hand in the air again to the same height as the statue's finger. Orange light. The finger glowed once again!

"No way!" Jill said out loud. "*Unlock destiny with the touch of a finger?* Well, here goes."

With that, Jill extended her left index finger and pressed it against the statue's. She was surprised to feel the finger was warm to the touch. When she moved to pull her finger away, Jill let out a short shout – she could not move it! It was stuck to the statue like a strong magnet sticks to metal. The stone became hot but the heat was not painful, the same sensation she felt by rolling her finger in wax made liquid by a burning candle. The longer Jill's finger was pressed against the statue, the brighter its finger became. Suddenly her finger fell free. Jill pulled it toward her, blew on it, and shook it in front of her face.

"Whew! What was that?" she exclaimed.

The finger of the statue remained orange, but it had changed in shape. It had, in fact, morphed like soft candle wax, and was now indented with the impression of Jill's very own finger. Jill could see the circles of her fingerprints distinctly in the orange of the waxy, indented finger of the statue.

All of a sudden Jill heard a loud crack, followed by a low humming, like a forest full of crickets at night. The arm of the statue fell limply to the statue's side. Shocked, Jill stepped back. The humming got louder and louder until it was a high pitched squeal, so loud and irritating that Jill had to plug her ears. Just as quickly as the humming started, it stopped. The room went very silent. No birds chirped. Jill did not dare make a noise.

Jill pulled her hands from her ears and looked around the room. Finally, she took a breath. As she did, a blinding light shone from the face of the statue and there was a loud explosion that knocked Jill off her feet onto the ground. Jill felt disoriented and numb, unsure what had happened. She moved to stand up, aware of a new level of light in the room. Jill could sense that she was no longer alone in The Atrium. There was some sort of presence in the room that felt very big and very, very close to her.

When Jill stood up she let out a terrible, blood-curdling scream.

"Little girl, you have no reason to be afraid."

In front of Jill stood the most amazing creature she had ever seen. Tall as two grown men, arms and legs thick with muscle, the being stood before Jill. The creature's skin was transclucent like ice that shone with flecks of gold. It's waist and legs were covered to the knees by a white robe, and a silver sash fell from its left shoulder across its chest and torso. The creature was neither a woman or a man; however, if forced to describe it, Jill would have said it looked more like a man. The moment she saw it, Jill knew the being wasn't human. It was something different, something magnificent, something other. The creature had what can only be described as hair which fell from its head in rivulets, curling toward its shoulders, the colour of fire.

Jill stood mesmerized when she looked into the creature's eyes. They were clear as crystal, and when Jill looked into them, she felt as though she became weightless, or left her body, or floated in the air. Her body felt the same way, numb and shaky, as when Mr. Kay disappeared into the picture in the kitchen. As she looked into the creature's eyes, she had the feeling that she looked into another world. The colour of the creature's eyes cannot be described, for, Jill saw as many colours as she spent minutes gazing into them. The eyes were like moving orbs, flecked with the energy of living colours. Greens alive like whole forests; blues as wild and deep as oceans where, beneath the surface, can be found newer more vibrant splashes and hues.

The being stood in front of the fish pond with an outstretched hand. Jill realized, with fear, that the statue had come alive, and now stared back at her!

"Whatever I did, I didn't mean to do it," Jill said quietly. "I'm sorry! I can be real clumsy at times."

"You did exactly what you were supposed to do. Now please, try to stand still."

With that the creature leaned down toward her and squinted its eyes. From its right eye came a bright light. Jill tried to close her eyes shut, but before she could blink, the creature's hands were framing her face, its fingers holding Jill's eyelids open. The creature shone the thin beam of light directly into Jill's right eye, and slowly moved the light across her entire eyeball. All Jill could do was stare back into the creature's astonishing face.

The creature pursed its lips, and pulled away from Jill. As it did, the beam of light disappeared.

"You did wonderfully." The creature smiled and removed its hands from Jill's face. "Fingerprint and retinal analysis complete. Identity confirmed. Welcome to The Atrium, Jill Strong."

Chapter Eight

“What just happened?” Jill asked, as if in a trance.

“You have been identified as Jill Strong, and you are about to receive something very valuable which you must protect at all costs.”

“You mean I found the treasure?”

“That you have, my child.”

“Where is it?”

“I am about to show you, although you have already seen it with your own eyes.”

Jill scrunched her nose and tilted her head to the side. She had already looked at the treasure?

“Come, sit at the edge of the pool, and look inside,” said the magnificent being.

Jill walked over the the wishing pond and sat on the raised stone edge.

“What do you see?”

“I see a large goldfish and some coins underneath the water,” replied Jill.

“You see correctly.”

"This is the treasure I've been asked to keep?"
The being laughed.

"You sound disappointed, but don't be. Not
everything is as it seems. Those things that seem to
have little value to us, might be the very things with
the most worth. We only need eyes to see the value
within."

With that, the being unfurled it's enormous
wings and raised them above its shoulders so that
they pointed straight up toward the ceiling. The
being doubled in height and loomed over Jill like a
tower.

"Please, Jill," it said, "touch the water with your
hand."

The being then stretched out its hands and tilted
it's head back, so that it gazed up at the ceiling.
Jill leaned over the pool and touched the surface of
the water with her right index finger. It was cool to
the touch. When her finger broke the surface of the
water, there was a rumbling sound. For a moment,
the whole room trembled. Ripples spread from the
point where Jill contacted the surface of the water
toward the outer rim of the pool.

"Careful now," said the being, "you might want
to step back."

Just as Jill stepped away from the pool, a great
geyser of water burst from its centre and shot
toward the ceiling. But the erupting water did not
fall back into the pool. Instead, it hovered in the air
until all the water had left the pool and collected
into a liquid cloud above the being's head. The
cloud threw out two liquid tentacles that attached

81

to each of the being's eyes. With a jolt, like it was being shocked, the being arched its back, and the cloud of water drained into the being through its tearducts. As the water entered the being's body, the colour of its skin slowly grew brighter, so that its whole body shone just like the glassy water-visor had, reflecting light before the being had a face. The being now looked even more astonishing.

The being folded its wings, turned, and looked back at Jill.

"I've waited for you to come for a long time, and as I waited I shed many tears.

The Keeper, as he promised, has brought you to me. My tears did not fall to the ground unnoticed. Now they have returned to me, and what once was sadness is now my joy."

"Why did you shed so many tears?" Jill asked.

"I feared, like many of my fellow seraphs, that my tears would run dry, and that you would never come."

"You were waiting for me?"

"That is why I exist, to help you accomplish the task given you by the Keeper."

"Wonderful creature, what should I call you?" Jill gasped.

"My name cannot be said in your language, it requires letters and sound that you cannot speak. Not yet, anyway. For the time being, you can call me Seraph, for that is what I am."

"Seraph, my name is Jill. It's good to meet you."

"The pleasure is all mine. Now, dear child, collect what is yours to keep."

Jill returned to the edge of the pool, now empty of water, and looked in. She was horrified to see a single goldfish, flapping about in the dry pool. It was an orange fish with white swirls and spots.

"Will it die?" she asked, turning to Seraph.

"It will not. Reach out your hand and touch it."

Jill did. She reached toward the fish and grabbed it by its tailfin. The moment she touched it the fish stopped moving, in fact, the fish was no longer a fish. Jill blinked a few times as though she was trying to get dust out of her eyes. But, when she looked again, the fish really was not a fish, it had changed into a small, orange and white pouch who's top was sinched shut by a red tasseled string. Jill picked it up and felt it between her hands. It was cool and metallic, sewn together by orange and white sequins in a pattern that looked very much like the scaling and colouring of the goldfish.

"This is where you will keep your treasure."

Jill turned to the seraph and scrunched her nose again.

"You mean to say that the coins at the bottom of the pool are the treasure I'm to keep?"

"You are right in what you say."

Jill frowned, then looked back into the pool. At the bottom of the now dry pool were ten coins, covered in dirt, and in need of a serious polishing. Jill hopped into the pool and one by one, picked each of the ten coins up and placed them in her open hand. Jill kept one in her hand and slipped the other nine into the little purse. She looked at the coin closely. Like the others, it was a dark grayish colour, covered all about in black, the way a glass candle holder darkens when the candle burns high. Jill rubbed her thumb over the coin to remove the dirt. On one side the coin was embossed with the same symbol sealed onto her letter and sculpted into the door handles of the Great Hall: the noble, magnificent horse. The other side of the coin, however, was blank. There were no markings at all.

The coin was quite heavy, the weight of a fifty cent piece, though it was smaller than the size of a quarter, and it was cool to the touch. Jill put it on the end of her thumb and tossed it into the air. The coin arced and flipped further away from her than she meant to toss it. Jill wanted to try a new joke with the seraph, a silly one she learned at school: "heads I win, tails you lose." But, Jill put too much sarcastic energy into her jest. She realized that the coin was out of her reach and that it would land just over the edge of the pool in the flowers and plants. Before Jill could move to try to catch it, the seraph threw out its hand, and in a flash, caught the coin before it hit the ground. Jill looked at Seraph sheepishly and smiled.

"Good catch," was all she could think to say.

"Jill!" Seraph responded not angrily, but sternly. "Though you may not yet recognize its value, this treasure is priceless. You must treat it with care. These are not just any coins. They are far more valuable than they seem. One day you will discover this truth."

"What don't I see? Why can't I know now?" Jill asked, impatiently.

"If you knew their value you would be too afraid to accept the task. For now it is better that you do not know. But some day, all things will become clear to you. All I can say to you now is that one man's treasure is another man's desire. The Keeper has enemies, foul creatures, who seek to steal and take from my Master what is rightfully his and his alone. The same is true of your coins. They are not safe, and will not be until they are brought to the Guardian at Terador. With him they must be hidden, and only then will their true value be revealed for all eyes to see. And yet, if you do not bring them to him, no one will ever know, and my joy will once again return to the earth in tears. Trust this treasure with no one; keep the treasure to yourself. There may be man or beast worthy of their trust, but if that trust is feigned, then your treasure will be lost." The seraph cupped Jill's chin in his hand and raised her head so that she looked him in the eyes. "What I have told you is overwhelming, I can tell by the look on your face. You must be of good courage, Jill, you must not be afraid."

Jill opened her mouth to speak, but could think of nothing to say. She scratched her head.

"Enemies? The Guardian of Terador? What do you mean? I don't understand."

"Of course you don't," replied Seraph, "but you will, Jill. You will."

"When?"

"When? I cannot say. And now I must leave."

"But you were sent to help me," Jill cried, frustrated once more and not afraid to let it show.

85

"I have given all the help I am able to give, at least for now. There is nothing left to say."

"That's what you think!" said Jill, rather loudly. "There is a lot more you could tell me. Like how I'm supposed to find this Guardian, and just who exactly he is.

Seraph leaned down toward Jill.

"There is one last thing I will do. You are tired and you must sleep. Before you do, I can impart to you some of my strength. You will need it if you are to fulfill your task."

Jill bowed her head and sighed, realizing Seraph would not answer any more of the questions burning inside of her. When she looked up, she stepped closer toward him and touched him with her hand. The seraph's eyes rolled into the back of his head and his body glowed with white light. A sudden, stiff shock of pain raced through Jill's entire body, as though she had been hit by some powerful force. Before she could yell out in pain, her body fell limp to the ground, and everything around her faded into black.

Chapter Nine

Jill woke to the sound of chirping birds and
gurgling water. Her body was so relaxed and
comfortable, she didn't want to move. Before she
opened her eyes she imagined she was lying in the
Great Forest on one of the beautiful mossy stream-
beds she had longed to lie on when she made her
way to the Great Hall. When she finally opened her
eyes, which took all the effort of her will for she
could have rested there for a long time, she found
that she was still in The Atrium lying among the
grass and flowers beside the pool.

"Seraph?" she said as she sat up from where she
lay and looked to the place where he earlier stood.
But he was no longer there. The room seemed much
bigger now that his huge presence no longer filled
The Atrium. In his place, however, was another
statue. A horse, young and strong, sculpted out of
stone, leaned its head into the pool which was once
again filled with water. There were fish swimming
about the pool, but no coins. When Jill saw there

were no coins, she automatically felt about for the orange and white sequined purse. It hung around her neck by the red cord.

"What's with all the horses?" Jill asked under her breath. "It'd be nice to see a real horse around here, you know." Jill sat on the ledge of the pool beside the horse's head. Its eyes were the same crystal as Seraph's had been, and the colour of the steed was glassy and reflective. Curious, Jill put her hand on the horse's forehead and whispered, "Seraph, is that you?"

Jill stopped her breath as she waited, half expecting the horse to shape shift in front of her into the majestic being. But it did not. The horse didn't move. It remained in the same position it had been carved out of the stone to assume, head over the pool, drinking from the water.

Jill stood up, disappointed but also amused. She wished she had been awake to see how the statue appeared, and what happened to Seraph. Jill imagined Seraph had gently picked her up and placed her on the soft ground beside the pool, then, unfurled his wings, looked to the ceiling, and with one dramatic movement pushed off the ground and disappeared through the roof. Jill ran to the windows overlooking the field and trees to see if she could see Seraph's powerful body charging through the clouds. She could not. Jill stayed at the glass for some time, mesmerized by the sky.

Finally, she turned when her stomach grumbled. She covered her murmuring stomach with her hand, embarrassed, a reaction she had performed many times during class before lunch at school. Jill blushed even though there was no one with her in the room. *I guess your stomach is trying to tell you something*, Jill thought. *Better go find some food.*

Jill left The Atrium but not before picking a few pieces of fruit from the trees: an apple, orange, and a mango which she planned to use in a fruit salad to eat alongside the other food she hoped to find in the fridge downstairs. She started to walk down the hallway toward the giant stairway. She stopped dead in her tracks when she saw that the door to the room marked *Private*, was cracked slightly open. Jill quickly stepped away from the door and stood with her back against the wall.

"There *is* someone else in the house," she whispered.

Jill looked around the hallway and tried to decide what to do. Was she safe? Was she in danger? Who was in the house? The Keeper and Mr. Kay had said nothing. nor had Seraph. Maybe they didn't know either. Jill realized she hadn't been imagining things when she looked through the little eyehole in the door. Whoever was in the house had one green eye. That was the only thing Jill knew for certain.

She stepped toward the door, planning to outrun whoever it was in the room if they weren't friendly, and hoping Mr. Kay or Seraph would help her if she needed it. "Seraph said not to be afraid." With that, a bit surprised at her sudden logic and courage, she put the fruit from The Atrium down, and knocked three quick raps of her fist against the wooden door.

"Hello? Is anyone here? I don't mean to disturb your privacy, but I just wanted to introduce myself." Jill heard a noise. The sound of wood scraping against wood. But, it didn't come from behind the door, it was an unmistakable kitchen sound: a chair being pushed away from the dining table. Someone or something was downstairs!

Jill turned from the door and started running down the hallway. She came to the stairs and grabbed onto the railing, as she started to descend the staircase, two steps at a time, the whole apparatus lit up in a column of light. Jill turned on her heel at the bottom of the stairs and started to make her way toward the kitchen. She slowed her pace to straighten her hair and tuck the bag of coins under her shirt. She took a few deep breaths once she was at the end of the hallway, then slowly, opened the kitchen door. No one. She scanned the kitchen. All eight chairs at the long wooden table were fixed in their place. Jill walked over to the table. Crumbs! And, a drop of milk. Jill, once again, quickly looked around the room. She walked behind the island that separated the eating area from the area where food was prepared, to see if someone was hiding behind it. Nothing. But she did notice a trail of crumbs along the floor.

The crumbs spotted the floor, here and there from the table, behind the island where Jill found a small piece of lettuce, all the way to the cupboard underneath the sink.

"I think I smell a rat," she said, loud enough to be heard. Jill reached up and grabbed a stainless steal pot that hung from the rack which was overtop the island. She gripped it in her right hand then slowly walked over to the cupboard.

"Whoever you are, come out slowly and quietly. I don't want to hurt you, but I will if I am forced to do it." There was no movement or sound. Jill waited. She counted thirteen heartbeats. "I know you're in there, you may as well come out. Don't make me force you. Come out slowly, or I'll use the weapon I brought with me from The Armoury upstairs."

Jill looked at the pot in her hand and rolled her eyes. "Come out!" she nearly shouted. With that, there was a sudden movement inside the cupboards and Jill heard a voice shout, "Don't hurt me! Don't! I'll come out! I'll stop hiding! I'll go, I'll go, just like he told me! Just don't do anything to me!"

"Out with you, then," Jill said with confidence that surprised her.

The cupboard door swung open. After a moment a foot shot out, followed by a leg, then the upper body and finally the head of a young, orange haired boy. He looked at Jill first with anxiety, then with wide-eyes of surprise. The boy was a little shorter than Jill. He wore brown corduroy pants, white sneakers, and a blue T-shirt with the number three on the front. The shirt was too short for the boy's body, and barely covered his little round tummy. The boy had freckles and very green eyes. He had crumbs all over his shirt, and a wet stain that went from his neck to his chest, like he had been sweating a great deal.

Jill started to giggle.

"What's so funny?" the boy asked self-consciously.

"Nothing," but then Jill burst into a laugh.

The boy squinted his eyes and frowned.

"Nice sword," he finally said, then smirked.

"What happened to you?" asked Jill, pointing at his shirt.

"You made me spill my milk."

"Do you normally eat your lunch in the cupboard under the kitchen sink?" Jill asked.

"Very funny."

Jill stopped laughing. She put the pot down, wiped her hand on her pant legs then offered it to the boy. "I'm Jill Strong."

The boy hesitated for a moment. "I'm Simon. Simon Henry Harris," the boy said automatically.

"I must say, Simon Henry Harris, I'm glad you're not a monster," replied Jill.

"And I'm glad you don't have a sword. I thought, maybe, you were that mean old Mr. Kay."

Jill laughed and Simon shook her hand.

"What's for lunch?" Jill asked.

"Turkey sandwiches with salt and vinegar chips," replied Simon.

"I'm starving," said Jill. "Why don't you grab your food from under the cupboard and we'll sit and eat at the table."

*   *   *

Jill and Simon ate a hearty lunch. Jill was amazed to find, when she opened the fridge, food that was already prepared, waiting to be consumed. When Jill told Simon about it he wasn't surprised.

"That's the way it always is. Breakfast, Lunch, Dinner, Supper. And snacks in between. There's always food in the fridge or the cupboards. "

"Always?" Jill asked. "And you said you've never seen the person who brings it? Who does all the grocery shopping?"

"I don't know. It's magic, just like the rest of the place. Who cares, really. It's really good food, and I'm happy to eat it," said Simon, taking a bite of his sandwich.

Jill looked down at Simon's stomach then back at Simon. "Looks like you enjoy it. How long have you been here?"

Simon sneered at Jill and pulled down his shirt. "I don't know, it's hard to keep track of time here. But, when I came, there was still snow on the ground. What month is it?"

"It's September. You've been here since the winter? Simon, you've been here for over half a year!"

Simon lifted his chin and looked at the roof. He counted out the months on his fingers. "Really, it's been that long?" Simon pondered. "Oh, but time is so different here.

It hasn't felt like more than a week. It's been wonderful."

"But didn't the Keeper leave you with a task or something to do?"

"Who?" Simon asked.

"The Keeper," replied Jill.

"The Keeper," Simon repeated. "I've heard that name."

Jill raised her eyebrow and looked at Simon. "What did he ask you to do?" she asked. "Did he give you a treasure too?"

Simon's eyes went wide, and he looked at Jill. "A treasure? No. What are you talking about." Simon was about to take another bite of his sandwich but stopped. "Were you given a treasure?"

Jill kicked herself for speaking about the treasure so openly. She didn't know Simon at all. She remembered the warning in the letter and forced a smile.

"Yes."

"What is it?" Simon asked. "Can I see it?

"I'm sorry," Jill replied, "but you can't. I've been asked to guard it, and can't show it to anyone else, until I go to a place called Terador."

"Hey, that's the place I'm supposed to go to as well," Simon said as he snapped his finger in recognition.

"Do you know anything about it?" Jill asked, almost frantically.

"Not much, but I think it's far away, and I know that I don't want to have to go there alone." Simon looked down at the table then quickly back at Jill. "My brother told me about it, the night he was taken away to the mines."

Jill sat upright in her seat.

"You have a family member at the mines, Simon?"

Simon looked away from the table and stared out the large glass door and out into the backyard. He was silent for awhile, and Jill started to wonder if he had heard her question.

"Three," he said to break the silence, in a barely audible whisper.

Jill closed her eyes and bit her lip. "Simon, I'm sorry."

Simon sighed. "I am too."

"How long have they been there?" Jill asked carefully.

"My father was taken first, three years ago, on my eigth birthday. My brothers were taken later, the night before I came here."

Jill looked at Simon for a long time, not knowing what to say. He sat quietly and gazed out the window. Jill felt very uncomfortable, she hated awkward silences when she felt like it was her turn to have something to say.

"You don't have to have anything to say, Jill," Simon said.

She smiled weakly.

"I don't think there is anything you could say. But maybe you could tell me something."

"What, Simon?"

"Who is the Keeper?"

"I don't know much about him. This house is under his care. I know that he is an important man. Someone I should very much like to meet. I knew it the first time I read his letter."

"Well," Simon said, leaning back in his chair, "if he's anything like his house, he must be amazing."

Jill sat and studied Simon's face. "Why haven't I seen you before, in the city?"

"What do you mean?" he asked.

"Your brothers, you have family members at the mines, that means, well," Jill cleared her throat, "that means your family has been disgraced, you're a *Shameface*."

Simon pushed up from his chair, it tipped over and hit the ground loudly.

"I don't see your veil anywhere, Jill! What are you trying to say?"

"No, I don't mean that, Simon. You're right. I have no veil, I wore one to escape the city, but that is the only time my face was hidden in Vendor. It's just that, if you're a Son of Disgrace, we might have seen each other at school, there aren't many of us, you know."

"Well I'd have you know that I'm not, Jill. You're the only Child of Disgrace in the room."

Jill instinctively pulled her hands to her face and looked away. Simon frowned. He bent over and picked up the chair, then put his hands in his pockets.

"But if I had stayed a moment longer in the city, I'm sure I would have become like you. My mother, my sisters, they found favour with the Council, they weren't covered in shame when my father disappeared. I'm sure they'll find a way to appeal to the Council and prove their innocence," Simon chuckled. "But with two sons at the mines now, they have their work cut out for them. Boy would I ever like to see the look on their faces if their veils were ever removed." Simon smiled wildly. He looked at Jill for a few moments, her hands still covered her face. "Don't be embarassed, Jill, I saw my sisters' faces all the time."

Jill looked up at Simon, astonished. "Really?"

"They took their veils off at home all the time."

"But, that's illegal – "

"Everybody does it, Jill. My sisters forced me to keep it on, though. I hated that stupid mask, it made eating so difficult."

"But what if a member of the Council were to stop by, or a Watchmen?"

"They don't care. They know it happens. The Council is only interested in a few groups of people, the people they're watching."

"How do you know all this?" Jill asked.

Simon stopped speaking and bent over to tie his shoe.

"I just know," he said. "Let's not talk about the Council anymore, Jill. You won't hear about it from me, 'for the Council alone' and all the other rubbish. I'm in the Forest for a reason." Simon stood up and started to walk to the sink with his dishes. He turned back to look at Jill after a thought and said, "Don't feel ashamed to show your face."

Jill looked back at the floor, but managed a weak, "Thank you, Simon."

Chapter Ten

Jill and Simon finished the dishes, not without a few laughs and splashes of water. Simon, slower on his feet than Jill after all the food he ate, was the wetter of the pair. When they finished, Simon started out of the kitchen.

"Where are you going?" asked Jill.

"C'mon," Simon said, "I want to show you something."

Simon walked down the hallway toward the staircase.

"Isn't this the most amazing thing you've ever seen?" Jill asked as they walked up the stairs. "It changes from wood to ivory. How do you think that happens?"

"Ah, you'll get used to it," Simon said flatly.

"How could I ever get used to something so, so magical?" Jill asked.

"Trust me. This is nothing. Wait until you see what I discovered."

They walked straight from the staircase down the hallway that led to The Atrium.

"Which is your favorite room?" Jill asked, curious.

"That's what I'm about to show you."

"There are so many to choose from," she continued. "I don't know if I ever could name a favorite. The Music room, The Library with all those books. I didn't know the world itself had so many books. I haven't even spent any time there at all and already I know it's one of my favorite rooms. Did you see the bookshelves? It would take weeks just to count all the books on them. How many more weeks would it take to read all of them?"

"I guess The Library would seem pretty amazing to someone who likes books. I think reading is boring."

"Boring?" Jill asked in amazement. Simon might have said he never learnt to swim, or couldn't ride a bicycle, or that he couldn't spell his own name. "You don't like to read? But reading is so fantastic. There are so many things to imagine when you read a book. Like what the main character really looks like, or if the characters speak in funny accents. There's always so many details authors leave out that the reader has to imagine." Jill lowered her voice and spoke as if she was sharing a secret. "Sometimes I wonder how and when the characters go to the bathroom."

Simon stared back at her blankly.

"What? Authors never write about that stuff. But if they're real people, well then they'd have to go to the bathroom, you know?"

As Jill continued to talk about books, Simon just stood and watched her. She was no longer walking but looking up at the ceiling and gesturing madly with her arms as she stood and went on and on about how important reading was. Jill's words slowly trailed off when she realized Simon was staring at her. "What, Simon?" she asked. "It looks like you've swallowed a lemon."

"You like reading too much. Don't tell me you're one of those people who grew up without a television."

"Television?" Jill asked, scrunching her nose. "What's that?"

"Are you serious!" Simon said, dropping his jaw. It was now his turn to show a little bit of surprise and disgust.

"I'm kidding. Simon, I'm kidding. Don't look at me like that. Of course I know what a television is, but only from reading about it in books. You're right. My mom didn't own a television, and my caretaker, well, let's just say my caretaker didn't have time for that sort of thing either."

"You've never watched TV! What planet are you from? You've never had to fight anyone for the remote control? You've never watched sports live on television? You've never seen cartoons? You're, well, you're like an endangered species. You're a," Simon coughed and tried to conceal a laugh, "you're a Dodo!"

"Very funny. I'm not a Dodo. I resent that. And what does it really matter if I've never seen a program on TV?"

"I guess I'm just surprised. I should probably ask for your autograph. Anyway, I think all that is about to change."

"What do you mean?"

"That's what I was about to show you," Simon said, with a gleam in his eye.

Jill crossed her arms over her chest and shifted her weight to her right foot.

"Just what exactly is in this room you're taking me to? If it's just a TV set, I think I'd rather go to The Library and read a good book."

"Hold your horses, Jill."

Simon took a few steps and stood in front of the door marked *Private*. He went onto his tiptoes, reached for the wooden sign, and removed it from the door. Underneath, in lettering like all the other signs on all the other doors read: The Media Room. Simon blushed a little and turned to look at Jill.

"I made this sign a little while ago, in case someone else came to the house."

"*You* made this sign? Simon, that's ridiculous. This isn't your home. This isn't your room."

"Oh, c'mon, Jill. It's no big deal. In a minute, maybe you'll understand why."

"What if the Keeper came and found you marking off your territory in his house?
Sheesh! What did Mr. Kay say?"

"Well, by that time, we weren't really on speaking terms. I'd rather not talk about him right now, thank you very much."

"What did you do to get on his nerves?"

"Hey, it's not a very difficult thing to do. He's a short tempered old grump of a man."

"Mr. Kay is a good friend of my family. He has been for a long time. Watch what you say about him. Anyway, he's probably listening," Jill warned, her voice suddenly dropping in tone.

"I hope he's listening. I'm just telling the truth. I thought he was nice too, until I made one little mistake."

"What mistake?"

"I ate the last piece of chocolate cake. *His* last piece of chocolate cake. It was when I first came to this place, before I knew his rules."

Jill laughed.

"What, you think that's funny?" Simon stuffed his hands in his pant pockets. "Oh, you can laugh, but just you wait. One of these days you'll eat the wrong thing or say something at the wrong time and make him angry. And he was going to teach me how to properly stuff a pipe, too. I don't expect that to happen anytime soon."

"Boys and their food! Well, put yourself in his shoes. Imagine you spent your life wandering from painting to painting. You'd probably cherish every opportunity you had for chocolate cake too."

Simon rolled his eyes. "Gee, I never thought of it that way, Jill. Thanks."

Simon pushed open the door and went inside.

"What's with the fruit on the floor?"

"Oh that," said Jill. "I was going to make a salad."

Jill followed Simon into the room. It was different then she expected it to be, empty save for some furniture along the far wall, a few couches and chairs with overstuffed pillows. The walls were painted black. In the middle of the room, just like in The Music Room, was a small table with a little box that had buttons on it. Simon stepped toward it.

"Careful with that," she said. "Make sure you read the manual."

Simon smiled. "Let me guess, you've already been to the Music Room. Don't worry, I know what I'm doing."

"What is it?" Jill asked.

"It's like a "Make your own movie" projector. It's kind of like in The Music Room only, the things you imagine here somehow get projected onto the walls, so you get to watch the adventures you make in your head on the walls all around you."

"What sort of things do you imagine?"

"Well, the day you came knocking, you interrupted an amazing car chase. A man wearing a black face mask had just robbed a bank, and he was being chased by the police in rush hour traffic in the downtown of a very large city."

"So you just watch the movie, you don't actually act in it?"

"Of course not, how would I act in it? It's just images on a screen, but it's way better than TV, because you can make it do whatever you want. It's just like The Music Room."

"But, when I was in the Music Room –"

"– here, let me show you," Simon interupted.

Simon leaned over the machine and pressed a button. Jill noticed that, like in The Music Room, there were no cords attached to the machine. It sat in the middle of the room, free from any electrical outlet. When Simon touched the button the machine glowed with soft yellow light. Jill realized she had mistaken the light from the machine for candles when she peered through the eyehole in the door. The walls suddenly lit up with blue light. The room had an eerie underwater feel to it.

"After you turn on the machine," Simon explained, "the rest is voice activated, you pretty much just tell the thing what you want to do. Something like this must be expensive. Probably a coupla million of dollars at least."

"Simon, are you sure you know what you're doing?"

"Trust me, okay. So Jill, what do you want to see?"

"Umm, I don't know?"

"C'mon. It's not hard. What's something you've always wanted to do? You were just going on about using your imagination outside in the hallway. Now you have a chance."

"I really don't know," Jill said.

"Well, what's something you've always wanted to see? Ever want to know what the beginning of a rainbow looks like, or see a cheetah chase after some prey? How about climb Mt. Everst?"

"Well, I guess I've always wanted to see animals in Africa."

"That's a good start."

Simon leaned over the machine and said: "African safari." The walls turned a darker blue then faded into black. The room was completely dark. Jill couldn't tell if her eyes were open or not.

"Simon?" Jill said out loud.

"Just wait, it only takes a second."

A small white dot flashed a few times in the middle of Jill's vision. Then, all of a sudden, Jill was staring straight ahead at a huge rhinocerous. The rhino nodded its head and stomped it's front right foot against the ground. Then, it let out a loud grunt and started running toward Jill. It came closer and closer toward the screen.

"Simon," Jill said nervously, "it's running toward us."

"I see that."

"Make it stop!"

"I'm not the one imagining it," Simon said, "you are."

"I am? No I'm not!"

"Yes you are."

The rhino was getting closer and closer, until finally it's face filled the entire wall. Jill closed her eyes and let out a scream.

"Jill, open your eyes and turn around. Look!" Simon said excitedly.

Jill did, and when she turned she saw the back of the rhino on the opposite wall, running away from them.

"It ran right through us," Jill said in a voice that Simon could hardly hear.

"No it didn't. The rhino was on the screen the whole time. He jumped from wall to wall, or TV screen to TV screen. In your imagination he ran right through us. Remember, Jill, you make it up in your mind. It's not real, you can't get hurt."

"Easy for you to say. I thought I was a goner."

Jill took a deep breath and looked at what she saw on the wall in front of her: a large plain, filled with long grass. In the distance she could make out the shape of two giraffes, slowly walking toward a watering hole where hundreds of flamingos stood, knee deep in water. Between her and the giraffes was a herd of wildebeests. Jill felt like she was standing right in the middle of a beautiful savannah.

"You're right, Simon, this is pretty amazing! I'm imagining this?"

"Yep."

"But, I'm not trying to. It's just there, like I'm just watching it."

"That's how it starts," Simon said. "It took me awhile to be able to actually notice I was the one putting those images up on the screen, but you'll get used to it."

"I don't know."

"Trust me. After awhile, it almost gets, I dunno, boring. It's almost anticlimatic to just watch it. I'm almost jealous of you. It's a challenge to imagine something totally new, to get that feeling of amazement you have right now. I've already imagined a safari before. Let's try something different."

"Okay. How about a coral reef."

"That sounds pretty cool."

Simon bent over and said *Coral Reef* into the machine. The room went instantly black, and in a matter of seconds, the white dot flashed, again, three times. Then, suddenly Simon and Jill were transported to a beautiful underwater world. Huge coral burst from the ocean floor like large plants reaching toward the surface of the water for air and light. Fish of every colour darted in and out of the coral. Clown fish, orange and white, appeared momentarily from the purple and white anemones they hid inside, then the fish slipped once again into the anemones' moving tentacles. Fish coloured blue, yellow and purple like parrots, with mouths that pointed out like sharp beaks, crunched on coral. Star fish sprawled about in the sand.

"Whoa! Look at that!"

Jill spun and looked where Simon was pointing. A huge hammerhead shark, moving its tail from side to side, carved a path in and out of sight between mounds of coral. Jill felt a sharp pain in her chest. Simon looked at her and said, "Breathe Jill." Jill exhaled loudly and realized she had been holding her breath. Simon chuckled.

"I know, it's hard at first. It feels so real, but you're not really in water, you're not really wet."

"It's beautiful," she exclaimed, "just like I imagined. Oh look, dolphins!"

The two turned and watched the dolphins appear like apparitions from the dark blue of the ocean deep, with fixed grins they jetted through the reef bobbing their heads.

"I've gotta say, Jill, you have a vivid imagination. I don't think I could imagine some of these colours if I tried. How are you doing it?"

Jill could only shrug her shoulders. The two enjoyed the underwater world, and after that, Jill imagined more. The moon and planets, Pluto, Venus, the beginning of a rainbow and the Himilayas. Jill asked Simon to say "endoplasmic reticulum" into the machine just to see if he could say it. But, she was also curious to see if the science books were true and how good her imagination worked with the machine, just how strong the magic was. Jill let out a gasp, amazed at what she saw. All of a sudden she stood with Simon in the middle of a microscopic world. Proteins and other substances she could not identify were the size of cars. What she guessed was the cell's nucleus was as big as an office building that other cell-parts, molecules and enzymes, parked in front of and interacted with.

"The schools in Vendor could use something like this," Jill said.

"It would definitely make Science class a lot more interesting," Simon agreed.

Jill and Simon traveled across galaxies and between valence layers of the smallest atoms, watching everything with a look of wonder, until Jill yawned. "Simon. What time is it?"

"I don't know," he said. "Why?"

"I'm exhausted. I think we've been at this for hours. I guess all this imagination has taken its toll on me. I need to sleep."

"Why don't you lie down on one of the couches over there against the wall. I moved them in here for that very reason."

"What are you going to do?"

"I'm going to stay here a little longer. I'm not tired. You've been the one imagining. End program." The red, fleshy chamber of the human heart Jill and Simon had been examining disappeared from the walls, and was replaced by the strange blue glow.

"I see why you like this room so much, Simon," Jill said. "The only thing that would make the room better would be if you could enter the world you imagine in your head. Now that would be unbelievable."

"That would be amazing. But it's also impossible."

"Oh well," Jill yawned. "Good night, Simon. Happy imagining."

With that, Jill went to the couch, curled her feet up into her chest, and fell fast asleep.

Chapter Eleven

The blue screens disappeared and were replaced by black walls. Jill waited for the little white light to flash, but it did not. *Perhaps you blinked and missed it*, Jill thought. It was hard to tell when her eyes were open and when they were not. Jill felt a sudden cold draft of air against her back. She turned to see if Simon had left the door open. As she did, she saw the flat vertical wall of a valley where she expected the door to be. She was alone, it was night. She stood on what once must have been an old streambed. Jill had no memory of the place but had a strange feeling she had visited it before.

A cold blue-white path of light was marked out in front of her by the waning moon. Jill stepped from the shadows toward the light. She was cold and shivering. As Jill stepped in the direction of the light she saw movement in the shadows around her. She stopped directly in her tracks and looked around. No movement. She slowly moved again, toward the light and saw the same movement, all

around her. Jill started to walk faster, hoping to get
inside the path of light where she would be able
to see better, but as she moved toward the light it
seemed to move away from her. When she stopped,
the movement stopped; when she moved a step
closer toward the light, the light seemed to move a
step away.

It was strange, but it seemed to Jill that the
movement she saw in the shadows was the movement of the shadows themselves, like giant black
theatre curtains moving in a forward direction
with a mind to envelop her, moving toward her
as she moved away from them, just as the light
moved away from her as she walked toward it, as
though she was on some strange tread mill, walking
forward, but constantly remaining in the same
place. Jill's initial fear turned quickly to frustra-
tion. She decided to stop and look up at the sky. The
moon was a sliver of light, a bone-coloured rip in
the fabric of the sky.

Movement again in the dark! Jill did an about
turn and looked directly into the darkness. All about
her shadowy figures were moving toward her. She
could not make out any of their features, but saw
they had glowing, green eyes. They walked slowly
toward her, metres away, whispering, growling
her name, telling her to stop trying to walk away,
inviting her to join them in the shadows.

Jill could feel her heart beat inside her throat.
She knew that if she stepped toward the shadows,
they would kill her. The creatures were within arms
length of Jill now, but came no further. She could

hear them breathe, the same deep-sounded purr of a sleeping cat. Jill knew she was safe on the fringes of light. The only thing that would keep the creatures from pouncing on her was the remaining light of the moon. Jill turned and started to walk briskly, still unable to move further in the direction she desired to go. Every step Jill made she feared the creatures would emerge from the shadows to harm her and steal the treasure she clutched near her throat. The whole time she walked, she felt like a large weight pressed down on her entire body so that her movement was slow, like she was trudging through deep snow without boots.

Abruptly, the groud before her fell away, and Jill had somehow come to the end of the valley. It dropped off into a sharp cliff. Jill looked up at the sky. Clouds were moving quickly and would soon cover the moon. Without understanding how, Jill suddenly knew that she was in mortal danger. It was then Jill heard the voice she would never forget, neither in her dreams or in the waking world, a voice that made her body numb and the hair stand on the back of her neck. At its sound, she felt the same feeling in her stomach that she had at school when Ms. Steinback scraped her nails across the chalkboard to get the class' attention.

"Darkness shall swallow the moon," the Voice said. "Swallow the moon and rule the night."

"Who's there?" Jill asked, frightened.

"Don't worry, little girl. When that cloud covers the moon, we shall meet."

"Who are you?"

"I've followed you long in your dreams, in the darkness, always out of reach.

From the time you were a young child I have searched for you, and at last have found you where he hid you, in this world. The shadow covering the past has finally caught you," the Voice said with a laugh that was quiet and cruel.

Jill hugged her arms around her upper body. She could sense that the Voice had moved closer. In the waning light she made out the shape of black, thinly parted lips that moved quickly with each sharply pronounced word. Behind the lips were large white teeth.

"You have something that belongs to me. I have come to take it back."

"What could I have that belongs to you?" Jill asked, and as she did, she held the coin pouch between her hands.

The Voice laughed again a gritty, scrapy laugh that made Jill's stomach churn. Jill looked up at the sky. The moon was almost fully covered by the moving cloud.

"This treasure has been entrusted to me and no one else. You will not touch it!"

Jill shouted.

Jill felt courage and strength surge through her body. She stepped toward the Voice, defiantly. As she did the cloud covered the moon, and the sky went completely black. Jill stopped moving. Her heart beat very fast. Jill heard hard clicks against the ground, like a dog's claws clicking against linoleum as it walks across a kitchen floor. The Voice was almost upon her. Suddenly Jill could hear and feel warm breath against her throat, then against the side of her cheek. Every muscle in her body tightened.

Jill tried to scream, but could not. Cold, scaly hands pressed tightly around her neck. Blood rushed to Jill's head as the hands squeezed around her throat. Her eyeballs bulged as Jill felt pressure swell between her temples, like she had been hanging upside down on the monkeybars at school for too long. In front of her was a pair of terrible eyes. The eyes were red in the centre, the colour of blood. Thin white veins spread from the red irises toward the edge of the eyeballs, which glowed yellow in the night. Jill felt as if the eyes burned through her. They were acidic and vicious.

"The treasure will be mine" the Voice said roughly.

Jill tried to call for help, but could not. She could taste blood in her mouth. Just when Jill thought she would black out, the hands released their suffocating grip from her neck and Jill dropped to the ground. A light, bright as a full moon, shone behind her. Jill heard the Voice scream, then heard the clickety sound of its claws, though much quicker now, trail away into the night. When she looked up, the Voice was gone.

"Jill."

Jill lay on the ground, quiet and still. Darkness once again surrounded her. She rolled toward the light, white and brilliant and warm like the sun. Eyes still closed, she sat up and slowly threw back her head, letting her body drink in the warmth of the light.

"Jill? Jill, wake up!"

Jill opened her eyes.

"Jill, it's okay. It's only a dream!"

"Simon?" Jill looked up at Simon, who was kneeling beside her, shaking her shoulders, shining a flashlight in her eyes. He had a concerned look on his face.

"What happened?" Jill asked, holding her hand to her forehead.

"I think you're the one who should tell me. From the looks of it, you've had quite a nightmare. You were walking and talking in your sleep, and everything."

"It was so real," she said. Jill sat up frantically, clutching her throat. "Where is it? Where is it!" she shouted at Simon, and looked frantically around the room.

"You mean this?" Simon handed her the orange and white bag that held the coins.

"What are you doing with that?"

"Easy, Jill, no reason to shout. You handed it to me in your dream. You were muttering something about a treasure. Then you handed it to me. Your eyes were open and everything. You looked like you had seen a ghost. I couldn't tell if you were playing a trick on me or not."

"I wasn't," Jill said, trying to sound calm, but not succeeding. She snatched the bag from Simon's hand, roughly. As she did, the bag dropped to the

115

floor, and the coins spilled onto the ground "Oh no!" Jill exclaimed.

Simon reached down to pick them up.

"No!" Jill shouted.

Simon stopped.

"Don't touch them! You can't. They're my coins. I'll get them."

"Alright Jill," Simon said cautiously, "just settle down, you're starting to make me nervous. You sound like my sisters all of a sudden. I can't be around you if you're like that, they're mean and unreasonable and make life a real drag."

Jill bent to the ground and started to collect the coins, counting each coin under her breath. Some of the coins were still spinning and turning in circles on the ground. She picked them up one by one and placed them in the bag.

"Wait, I've only got nine! There were ten. Simon! Where's the other one? You haven't gone and stolen one, have you?"

"Of course not!" Simon responded. "Really, Jill, what's gotten into you?"

"Look! Over there. It's rolling toward the wall."

Jill moved toward the coin which was turned on its side, rolling in the direction of the wall where the image of an enormous Ferris wheel was projected. The wheel was larger than any one Jill had ever seen. It spun in the middle of an amusement park that was set in a bay by the ocean. The outermost part of the Ferris wheel hung over the water.

"Don't worry Jill," Simon assured, "the coin will stop once it hits the wall. Take it easy, will you?"

Jill stopped and watched with Simon as the coin rolled, about to make contact with the wall. But, instead of hitting the wall, spinning on its side, and stopping on the floor as Simon expected it to, the coin kept rolling, then disappeared.

"Where did it go?" Jill exclaimed.

Simon stood looking at the wall, dumbfounded.

"It went into the wall," he said in a tone of fascination. "Look, there, do you see it, it's falling! It's entered the scene I was playing in my imagination and it's falling!"

No sooner had Simon finished saying so, then the coin landed on one of the spinning Ferris wheel's seats.

"Make it stop spinning, Simon. I can't lose that coin!"

Simon turned toward the machine in the middle of the room and yelled: "Program stop! End program!" Nothing happened. He leaned closer to the machine and yelled again. Nothing.

"It's not working, Jill."

"Oh no!" she moaned. "What do I do?"

"How important is it?" Simon asked her.

"What?"

"How important is the coin, Jill?"

Jill looked at Simon. "It's priceless. Ah!" she screamed as the Ferris wheel continued to spin. "What do I do?"

"We have to go after it," said Simon.

117

"Go after it! How?" she asked.

"Do exactly what the coin did, go up to the wall and enter the screen."

"That's impossible!" Jill said. Jill suddenly remembered Mr. Kay, and her experience watching him in the kitchen. "It looks like Mr. Kay couldn't have given me a lesson too soon."

"We better go now, Jill. Once that coin reaches the top of the Ferris wheel, it's going to fall into the water. Look how those seats tilt when they start to make their way down the other side of the wheel."

Simon grabbed Jill by the hand and pulled her toward the wall. "Here goes nothing," he said.

"I don't know how this works," said Jill, "but we need to get onto that seat.

Hurry!"

With that, they both stepped toward the wall, yelling at the top of their lungs. As they did, they put their hands up to protect their faces from impact should their efforts be unsuccessful. They didn't need to protect their faces. Simon and Jill suddenly found themselves clutching onto the side rails of a white Ferris wheel carriage, more than fifty feet off the ground, still yelling, but otherwise unharmed. Simon, realizing he was okay, looked around and then abruptly stopped yelling. He looked at Jill who, realizing he was no longer yelling, stopping shouting as well.

"We did it, Jill, we're in my imagination!"

Jill frantically looked all about the carriage. "Look Simon, we're not in the right carriage. The coin isn't here!" Jill looked at the other cars. "Oh no! There!"

She pointed to a carriage that was two seats below and behind them. Jill quickly looked over her shoulder in the other direction. They were starting to make their way toward the top of the wheel! Soon they would start the descent.

"Jill, don't!" Simon said, reaching for her as she stepped over the rail to hang herself over the carriage.

"I have to get that coin. Seraph told me to guard it with my life."

"Well, you might lose your life if you go after it," Simon reasoned.

Jill ignored Simon and kept moving. She dangled her body from the rail. Her shoes hung a few feet from the roof of the carriage below.

"Careful Jill!" Simon urged.

"Shh! I need to concentrate." Jill steadied herself until she was hardly moving, then let go of the rail.

"Jill!" Simon shouted as she let go of the rail and dropped away from the carriage.

She landed on top of the carriage, which wobbled back and forth. Jill anticipated the movement and in a swift motion grabbed onto the end of the roof, which, thankfully, raised at the edge into a solid metal bar. Jill swung her feet over the roof and into the carriage. She looked up at Simon and smiled. He shook his head. Jill took a deep breath, grabbed onto the handrail, and started to climb over it.

119

"Jill, you'd better hurry!" Simon warned.

Jill looked up. Simon, in the carriage above, would soon start his descent over the other side of the Ferris wheel. Jill steadied herself and aimed. She landed on the roof, but, in her haste, hit it much harder than she had previously landed. The carriage swung violently and Jill had to use all her strength to grab the edge of the roof just to hang on. As she did, her body slid, and dangled over the edge. She looked down past her feet and saw cement and water. She barely kept hold, the weight of her body pulling mercilessly at her fingers which gripped the rail.

"Jill, are you okay?" shouted Simon.

"The coin!" she yelled back.

For, as she hung from the roof, clutching onto it for dear life, she also watched the coin teeter on the edge of the carriage seat. The impact of her body against the roof had moved the coin. Jill watched, as if in slow motion, as the coin teetered on the edge of the seat. She kicked her leg up and got a foothold on the handrail. Once she was able to put weight on her foot, she removed one hand from it's grip on the roof and grabbed the back of the seat. Jill swung inside. As she did, the carriage started to make its descent over the water. Jill lunged for the coin as it fell toward the metal floor grate.

She was too late. Before she could catch it, the coin slipped through the floor grate, hit the back of the carriage below it, and spun in an arc toward the water. Jill let out a cry as she watched the coin hit the surface of the ocean with a small splash and then disappear. She pressed her forehead against the handrail and looked vacantly at the water below.

"Well Jill, you've done it. You've gone and done the one thing the Keeper insisted you do not do. It's hardly been twenty-four hours and you've lost a coin," she said to herself.

Jill lightly banged her head against the rail a few times. Then she sat up. She kneaded her knees with her hands and looked up at the sky. She shook her head in disbelief. "And, you got your wish. Somehow you've entered the world of imagination.

Now the question is, how are you going to get yourself out?"

Chapter Twelve

"**J**ill?" Simon shouted. "Are you okay? Did you get the coin?"

Jill lifted her head and looked toward Simon where he sat two carriages ahead, below her. "I didn't get to it in time. I'm afraid I've really lost it."

"What do we do now?"

"We have to get off this thing."

"And how do we do that?" Simon shouted back.

"I don't know. You were imagining the wheel when I woke up. Do you think that you can imagine stopping it?"

"I guess I could give it a try."

Simon sat down in his seat and covered his face with his hands. He leaned against the handrail of the carriage and tried to picture in his mind the Ferris wheel come to an abrupt halt. He muttered *Stop moving, stop moving* over and over under his breath. He heard a loud creak then the sound of scraping metal. Simon listened for a moment.

"Jill, I think it's working. Did you hear that sound?"

Before she could answer, Simon's carriage suddenly dropped and he was thrown forward in his seat.

"I don't think so, Simon. It looks like the wheel is speeding up," Jill replied. "We're moving faster than before. Hold on!"

The Ferris wheel started to spin faster each time it made a full rotation. Jill and Simon in their separate carriages climbed up the wheel and dropped down the other side at a much faster rate. Soon, their vision was a blur of ground, water, and sky.

"Ohhhh!" Simon yelled, "I think I'm going to be sick!"

But Jill could not hear him. She could only hear the hollow sound of wind and air as it rushed passed her face and blew her hair all about the carriage. There was a sudden loud snap, like the crack of a very large whip, and then total quiet. Jill opened her eyes. The wheel had broken completely free of its bearings and had been catapulted from the concrete landing out over the water! The entire structure was in mid air. Jill could do nothing but brace herself for the impact the giant wheel would momentarily make with the water. She held onto the rail and shut her eyes. *Oh Keeper,* she found herself thinking, *help!*

Jill felt dizzy as she realized the spinning came to a stop. She waited to hit the water, for the sound of the foamy splash as the wheel hit the surface, but it did not come. Jill slowly openend her eyes. She was still in the seat of the Ferris wheel, which was suspended in the air. Jill assumed the wheel had not stopped and that her senses and reflexes had been heightened in the moment of trauma so that everything appeared to happen in slow motion. Jill remembered reading that time often seemed to slow down to people involved in terrible autowrecks and other sorts of accidents. To her surprise, Jill heard a voice behind her, calling her name.

"Jill! Hurry, we don't have much time."

Jill turned, and saw the last thing she would have expected to see. Her heart leapt at the sight of it, the closest thing to joy and relief she had ever experienced. Seraph hovered outside the carriage behind her, his great wings moving in the air. With his right hand he motioned for Jill to come to him. Under his left arm he held Simon, who was unconscious. Jill moved toward the edge of the carriage and jumped. Seraph caught her and pulled her to his chest. He felt solid and strong as a giant rock.

"Seraph! You came! You came to help me."

Seraph kissed her forehead and smiled. Then, in a swift motion, he flapped both wings, and the three went sailing high into the air. Seraph told Jill to look down. As she did, the giant Ferris wheel hurtled toward the ocean. When it hit the surface of the water great white waves burst all around the wheel. Carriages and metal pieces were thrown upon impact beyond the wheel into deeper water. Some landed onto the nearby beach. Jill felt sick to her stomach. She couldn't help but imagine what would have happened to her and Simon had they been in the wheel when it hit the water.

"Child, you asked for help at just the right time," Seraph said.

"Where did you come from, Seraph?" asked Jill. "How did you hear me?"

"I was sent to you. I came from the Great Hall."

"Where are we?" asked Jill. "How did we get here?"

"You are in one of the lands beyond the Great Forest," replied the seraph.

"But how did we get here? One moment I was in the Great Hall, and suddenly we were, well, we were *here*," Jill said, "pointing at the water."

"The Keeper has many lands under his care, and, there are many ways to get to them. You've discovered one of them."

"Oh, but it was all an accident," said Jill. "We didn't mean to. It was all a mistake, a stupid, stupid accident. I didn't trust Simon when I should have, and I was careless with the treasure, and now I've gone and lost a coin."

Jill looked away from Seraph and started to cry. She hated herself for doing it; she never cried in front of others. She felt foolish and afraid to show emotion so openly on her face: in Vendor it was a dangerous thing to do, punished with a swift crack of a disciplining stick by her teacher Ms. Steinback or some other adult. Seraph pulled Jill into his chest and comforted her. When Jill opened her eyes, Seraph was standing on the shore of the bay. With one foot he stood in the water, the other was on dry land. He held both children in his arms.

"Child, do not fear. It will be alright. When you make mistakes, you learn from them. But know this: in the Keeper's lands there are no accidents, and even misfortune can be changed into something great."

"Oh I wish that were true! But I can't imagine how. Seraph, please take us back to the Great Hall."

"I am sorry Jill, but that I cannot do."

"What? Why not?"

"You asked for help, and I gave it to you. I have fulfilled my duty, I rescued you from the terror of the wheel, and now I must leave you."

"You can't! You can't leave Seraph, I *need* you."

"Child, you will be alright. You have all the help you need," he said, lifting the unconscious Simon up with his arm.

"But, but we need to get back to the Hall so we can travel to The Guardian at Terador."

"Do you not yet see, child? That journey has already begun," Seraph replied. "From this beach you will find your way. Before you leave it you must recover the coin."

"Seraph, it's gone! You must not have heard me. The coin is *gone*. It fell into the water. How can it be recovered?"

Seraph said nothing. He winked at Jill and smiled.

"Seraph? Seraph!" Jill said as he slowly bent over and put Jill on the ground. He then gently lay

Simon, who started to moan and move his head, onto the sand.

Without another word, Seraph put his right hand over his heart, looked up to the sky, and disappeared into thin air. Jill stepped toward him as he disappeared, trying to grab hold of him, but she only grabbed at air. She stood motionless for some time, staring at the empty space Seraph moments earlier occupied.

Jill was torn from her troubled reverie when Simon rolled onto his side in the sand and slowly sat up. Simon rubbed his eyes and yawned. He looked out over the water then up at the sky. He looked over toward the bay area where the Ferris wheel once stood, then he looked at Jill where she stood on the beach. Simon stared at her with wide eyes.

"Jill?"

"No Simon, you're not seeing a ghost. It's me."

"Did we –" he started to say, then pointed up at the sky.

Jill nodded her head.

"And then it –" he said, and pointed at the water.

Jill put her hands on her hips and nodded again.

"And now we're –"

"Now we're here," Jill finished.

Jill explained what happened while he was unconscious. Simon exhaled loudly and lay back down in the sand. He stared into the sky and said, "I thought I was dead. I thought it was all over. My short little life, over just like that," he said as he snapped his fingers.

"Yeah, well, near death experiences seem to be a new theme in our lives, what with dreams and all."

"That can't be very good for our health," Simon said, rubbing his neck.

"No, I don't think it can be," Jill agreed. Jill stood in the sand and was quiet.

"This isn't normal, Jill. Something happened. How did you do it?"

Jill looked at Simon, puzzled. "Do what?" she asked.

"Bring us here," Simon responded.

"Bring us here? What do you mean, Simon? It was your imagination flashing up on the screen in the Media Room, not mine, remember?"

"Yeah, but I heard you say it before you went to sleep."

"Heard what?" Jill asked.

"Don't look at me like that, Jill. I heard you. You said it would be real neat if we were able to enter the world of our imagination. Don't you remember?"

"That? I was just talking out loud, Simon. I didn't mean I wanted to lose a coin and leave the Great Hall to be stranded in some strange land!" Jill looked at the wreckage from the Ferris wheel that was strewn about on the beach and shuddered.

"Well it looks like you got your wish. My sisters always used to say 'Careful what you wish for.' I can't believe I'm saying it, but it looks like they were right." Simon was quiet for a moment. "There's something strange about this, Jill, and I can't quite say what it is."

"What do you mean?" Jill asked.

"You. You have some strange power. You're like *him*." Simon pointed with his head toward the water. Jill turned and looked behind her.

"Who, Simon?"

"Mr. Kay. He could slip in and out of worlds. You must be magic too."

Jill laughed. She stopped laughing when she saw that Simon was being serious.

"Magic? What do you mean, Simon? That I'm some sort of witch or fairy? Look at me, do you see a magic wand?"

"Well, how do you explain this?" Simon said lifting both arms in the air.

Jill thought for a moment, then sat down on the sand. She pulled her knees into her chest. "Well I sure hope not."

"But it would be so cool to have some sort of magic power, Jill."

"Look at you, you're already forgetting where we come from, Simon. I'm a Daughter of Disgrace, remember? Isn't that bad enough? You know what they'd do to me if they found out I knew some magic." Jill shuddered.

"But you're just a kid," Simon reasoned. "And that was such a long time ago."

"They killed children too. They would do it again."

"Even for magic like Mr. Kay's?" Simon asked.

"I don't know," Jill replied.

"It seemed so fun and adventerous. Not dark or evil." Simon grabbed fistfulls of sand and let the fine substance sift through his fingers and disappear in the wind. Jill watched him for awhile.

"I don't know, Simon. If I got us here, I'm sorry, and it was an accident. Mr. Kay said that it was possible to learn how to move from world to world, or picture to picture. I must have done something accidentally that made it happen."

"Or said something." Simon's eyes suddenly went wide. "Maybe someone heard you."

"Simon, you're creeping me out. Who could've heard me?"

Simon hesitated. Finally, he asked, "What went through your head, Jill? What were you thinking the moment you stared death in the face?"

Jill blushed and looked at the ground. Simon turned his head and watched her. "Everything was so slow, and quiet, and clear," Jill said. "I thought of my mother.

I remembered how beautiful she was. I felt sad that I would die so young and that I'd lost the treasure. It was only a moment, but I thought those things. But more than anything, I felt I had disappointed the Keeper. I don't know him, but the thought of not actually doing what he asked me to do made me feel more sad than I have ever felt."

Jill looked at Simon and smiled. "Is it a strange thing to want so badly to please someone you have never met?" she asked. "Someone you hardly know anything about?"

Simon sat up. He picked a rock from the sand and tossed it into the water. "I don't know. It does seem odd, but I had similar thoughts. I didn't think about my family, not even my sisters," he smiled wryly. "I didn't think about Vendor, not even the pain my body would feel greeting death. All I thought about was that by not meeting him, I'd be missing a great adventure."

"But, we made it," Jill brightened.

"We made it. And now I'm sure of something."

"What's that?" Jill asked.

"I'm alive," Simon said squinting his eyes, "and before I die, I would like to meet him."

"Careful what you wish for," Jill repeated, half joking. "Do you think he heard me? You think he somehow brought us to this strange place?"

"If he didn't, he now knows that we're here."

Chapter Thirteen

S imon stood up and brushed the sand off his trousers. The two looked around. To the north was the amusement park. It looked smaller than it once did, now that the Ferris wheel was gone. The park was set upon a plot of land that rose out of a steep rock face standing more than ten metres above the water. The grade of the rocks diminished at a gradual angle into shoreline nearly half a kilometre south of the park where Jill and Simon stood on the beach. The beach had warm golden sand and stretched behind the children for about a hundred metres. The water was directly to the east. Simon pointed this out, noting that the sun was just rising from that direction to the highest point in the sky. The stretch of beach was bordered to the south and west by trees, and rocky terrain that rose into the small cliff on which stood the amusement park in the north.

"Seraph said we were not to leave the beach without the coin," Jill noted.

"Do you think it could have washed up onto shore?"

"The waves are fairly large," Jill said, "but I don't see how that's possible. It bounced off the Ferris wheel and landed in the water all the way over there by those rocks."

"Well, we may as well start looking," Simon concluded.

They decided to start in the shallow water by the shore. They both took off their socks and shoes and walked up to their ankles in the water. They walked up and down the stretch of beach, looking into the murky water intently. They found nothing. They stepped out of the water, rubbed their necks which were strained from keeping their heads down for so long, then started to walk along the shoreline in the same manner: side by side, eyes scanning directly at the area in front of their feet as they walked. When they came to one end of the beach, they would step a few feet away from the water, then walk in the other direction, always carefully scanning the ground, in hopes of spotting the silver coin.

After quite some time, Jill stopped walking. "Simon, this is useless. We're already more than ten metres away from the water, and still no coin. The waves aren't that large. How could the coin have made it this far inland?"

"You're probably right. Maybe we should start back at the water and retrace our steps. We might have missed it."

"We could go on doing this forever and never find it," Jill said. "We don't even know if it's here. It's like looking for a needle in a haystack."

"Well, what else can we do? You know what Seraph said."

"I know," said Jill. "How did Seraph ever think we could find it?"

"Wait a minute!" Simon announced, "what's that?"

Simon pointed to a spot in the sand a few steps behind Jill. Jill turned and looked but saw nothing.

"What is it Simon? I don't see anything."

"You have to look at the right angle, you need to see the reflection of the sun.

Move your head a bit."

Jill did. She tilted her head from side to side, then stepped to where Simon was standing and squinted her eyes. There! A silver glimmer of light reflected out of the sand. The two looked at each other and then ran toward the spot. Jill and Simon dropped onto their knees into the beach. They looked down on a thin arc of silver sticking out of the sand. Jill smiled at Simon.

"Good eye."

She was about to reach her hand toward the silver object, but stopped abruptly when she heard a sound that seemed to come from behind her, and above her, and all around her. A voice. Jill gulped.

Be careful little eyes what you see!

Jill looked wide eyed at Simon. They heard the voice again.

"What was that?" Simon stood up and looked around. "Who's there?" he said, and spun on his heels.

A strong wind came with sudden force from the ocean and blew across the beach. It blew sand all about, in the children's eyes and mouths. The water was choppy and violent. White waves breached and foamed. The sand bit into their skin. Simon crouched back onto the ground. The wind continued to blow.

"What's happening?" he shouted toward Jill.

"I don't know. Oh no," she cried above he sound of the howling wind. "The coin!

It's been covered by the sand. We have to find it!"

The two moved over the spot where they last remembered seeing the coin and frantically dug about, scooping sand with their hands blindly as sand swirled around their bodies and blew in their faces. Jill felt something metallic under her fingers. Face near the sand, she squinted in the wind at the beach and saw a thin line of silver.

"I've found it," she yelled toward Simon.

As she yelled, the wind abruptly stopped. There was an eerie silence. Simon looked at the water, which was now totally still.

"I don't have a very good feeling about this place, Jill. Grab the coin, and let's run for the trees."

Jill brushed sand away from the thin line of silver with her finger.

"What is this?" Jill gasped. "It looks like a coin, but it's different somehow." Jill dug a little more around the metal, then jumped back and screamed.

"What Jill?" Simon asked in surprise.

"Simon, this isn't a coin, it's a ring!"

"Yeesh, Jill. I thought you saw something worth screaming about. What's the big deal?"

"The ring is still attached to a hand!" Jill announced.

"What do you mean? Jill, you must be imagining things."

Simon bent over the metal, and blew sand from it with his mouth. The force of the air from his lungs pushed more sand away to reveal what Jill feared – a long white finger!

"Jill, was there anyone else on the Ferris wheel with us?"

"I don't know. What do you mean? You think there were other people on the ride?"

"If there were," Simon continued, "could they have been thrown this far from the wheel?"

"It was spinning pretty fast," Jill said. "I don't know. Oh!" Jill dropped to her knees again and started to frantically pull sand from the finger along with Simon. In a matter of seconds they had exposed the rest of the hand. Soon they had uncovered a forearm. The hand and forearm were strangely white, like skin with no pigment.

"Simon, stop! Look!"

"What?"

Jill pointed at the hand. "The hand, it just moved!" They both froze and watched the hand. It lay completely still. Jill looked at Simon, the blood completely drained from her face. "I know what I saw, Simon. The hand moved."

Simon leaned in closer to the hand. He quickly touched the hand and then pulled his arm away, like he was testing to see if a clothes iron was hot. But the hand was not hot. It was cold, like he was touching a raw piece of chicken pulled from the refrigerator, ready to be cooked. Simon touched the hand again. He lifted the ring finger.

"I don't think so, Jill, this hand is deathly cold. I don't think there is life in it."

The words were hardly out of his mouth when suddenly the hand shot up out of the sand and gripped Simon by the wrist. Jill screamed as Simon's hand was pulled forcefully against the sand. The white hand tightened around Simon's wrist. Simon tried to pull away, but the grip was stronger than iron.

"Jill, help!"

Suddenly, another hand emerged from the sand, exposing a white forearm, bicep and shoulder. The other hand reached toward Simon, groping along the sand, then his arm until it stopped at his chest. The arm hooked itself around Simon's neck and pulled him against the sand. The ground began to shake. Jill fell back into the sand away from Simon and the hands. The sand all about Simon started to drop and fall away, like sand falling through the hole of an hourglass. An area, not much longer than Simon's body, began to sink away into the ground.

Jill crawled to the edge of it and peered down. Simon was about three feet below her.

"Simon!" she yelled. "Grab my hand!"

Jill reached down to Simon. He feebly thrust out his arm and tried to grab Jill's hand, but he couldn't. He kept sinking further and further into the ground. Sand from the higher ground, along the edges of the sinkhole started to pour in and fill the hole. The sand was burying Simon! Simon was disappearing into the ground fast, he was nearly covered in sand. Jill could no longer see the terrible white arms. Simon was coughing and shouting incoherently.

"Simon!" she yelled again. "Simon!"

The ground continued to rumble and sink. And then, Simom's head disappeard beneath the surface of the sand. Without thinking Jill threw herself at the sinkhole, jumping toward it, desperate to save Simon. But, her fall was stopped short by level ground. The sinkhole had been replaced by solid ground again. Simon was gone.

* * *

Jill stood looking at the sand all around her, worried that her next step would be into another sinkhole and that she, too, would be pulled underground and disappear. Jill was shocked and frightened.

"Forget the coin, Jill," she said out loud. "Simon was right, you need to run for the trees."

Motivated less by courage and more by terror, Jill ran for the trees as fast as she could. She didn't

stop running until she could no longer see sand.
Then, she found a fallen tree, sat down, and cried.
After some tears, she felt a little relieved, though
still afraid and disoriented. She still did not know
where in the world she was. Was it the real world or
somewhere in Simon's imagination? Yet, how could
she be in Simon's imagination if he was, if he was
– she could not think it. She would not think it. She
would never say it until she knew it was true. If that
man or creature could live in the sand, then Simon
could too. Jill dropped her head onto her knees in
despair, and started to cry again.

Her cries were interupted, by voices that spoke
in unison.

"Little girl, why do you cry?"

Jill stood up with a start. She looked around
her. All she saw was forest on every side. But the
sound of the voices echoed in her head. The voices
were low pitched and haunting. It was like standing
in the middle of a stringed instrument section of
an orchestra that was playing low notes in the bass
clef.

"You cry for your friend who has disappeared,"
the voices said, together.

"Who said that?" Jill asked looking all about.

"Keep looking, but you won't see us –"

"Where are you?"

"Keep searching but you will not find us. We
cannot be seen."

"Honestly," Jill said, exasperated. "It must be
my fate to be haunted by voices."

"Not more haunted than we are, young girl. Be thankful that you can hear. Be thankful that you can be seen. We are not so fortunate as you."

"Who are you? Please, you're scaring me," Jill said.

"The question, better put young girl, is, 'Who are you?'"

"My name is Jill Strong. I'm not afraid to tell you who I am. Now please, tell me who you are!"

The voices were silent for sometime, then Jill heard the sound of a low murmuring, as though the few voices were speaking softly, the way a fly sounds when it buzzes against a window, or the way a child sounds when he counts against a wall in a game of hide-and-go-seek.

"Did you say Jill *Strong*?"

"Yes. That is my name. I am Jill Strong. Now who are you?"

"We are ones who know that name. Child, we were friends of your mother."

Jill relaxed her body a little. "You knew my mother? How? When?"

"Daughter of Grace, your questions will be answered, but they must wait. You are not safe. This is a dangerous land. It belongs to the Dark Prince, though he is known by other names. We must find somewhere else to talk, somewhere that is safe. He roams these lands and has many foul creatures who do his evil work. There are few in these woods that can be trusted."

Jill gulped and looked back at the beach.

"My friend! My friend Simon. The boy I came with. The boy with me on the sand!"

"Fear not, child. The boy is alive, but what his condition might be is not ours to say. If the seed that was planted in the sand was good, then he will meet a good fate. However, if the seed planted was not good, if it was a tare or weed, then –"

The voices stopped.

"Then what?" Jill asked.

"Then," said a single voice that sounded like a sad, lonely violin, "then his life is in great danger."

"What do you mean? I don't understand."

"There will be time for understanding later," said the lonely voice, "but you must come with us, Jill. You must trust us. I know it is difficult. You cannot see us. But we can only offer you our word, and, our protection."

Jill bit her lip as she looked to try to see where the voice came from. All she could see was the forest. She could feel a presence, but could see no one.

"Where are we going?" she asked.

"Hold out your hand. We will lead you there."

Jill did not know what else to do, so she hesitantly lifted her hand out in front of her. Her hand shook the way it shook when she had to read in front of all her classmates at school. Jill felt a sudden, warm pressure against her wrist. She tried to pull her arm back towards her body but could not. Her hand was now being held in the solid grip of another, invisible hand. Jill looked at her hand

and then focused her attention at a spot a little ways above it.

"You're real!" she said, relieved. "You aren't ghosts?"

Jill heard laughter, she guessed there were at least two other beings accompanying the creature that now held her hand.

"Yes, Jill, we're real. Real as the trees," said the single voice again.

Jill was pulled into the air. She let out a yelp of surprise. Her feet dangled off the ground, and she continued to be pulled higher in the air. Soon she felt pressure around her waist. Her arm dropped freely to her side. She was being lifted by invisible hands that now held her around the waist. She was about two metres in the air.

"Jill, I'm going to set you down now."

Jill felt something firm underneath her.

"Relax a little bit Jill, you can sit here," said the disembodied voice. "You'll be safe, just hold on, I hope you're okay with flying."

"Flying?" Jill asked hesitantly. "I've never flown. I've never been in an airplane or a helicopter. I'm not sure I can – whoa!" Jill yelled.

"It's okay."

Jill fell forward and was stopped by something hard in front of her. She reached out her arms and found that she could wrap them around it. It was thick as a tree trunk but warm and soft like a goose-down pillow.

"Yeah, okay, you can hold on Jill, but not so hard. You're choking me."

"What?"

"Jill, you're choking me."

"Oh, sorry." Jill blushed and loosened her grip around the invisible creature's neck. "So," Jill asked, "do you have a name?"

"Yes, I do. You can call me Stelton. Here we go."

In a matter of seconds Jill was high above the ground and slowly moving higher and higher until she was level with the treetops.

"You're less likely to be spotted here among the tops of the trees. The Dark Prince probably forgets that we can fly. It's been so long since he's seen any of us. So long since we've seen ourselves."

"The further Jill flew, the thicker the forest became. Soon she could not see the forest floor, only the tops of the trees. Jill turned and looked behind her. The rock cliff where the Ferris wheel once stood was a small speck in the distance. Jill could see the shoreline vaguely against the blueness of the sky where the sun was at the peak of its arc.

On and on they flew, until they came to a large rock formation that spiked out of the forest of trees. The rock was shaped like a cone whose top had collapsed inwardly on itself.

"A volcano!" Jill announced.

"A dormant volcano," said Stelton. "The last time it spouted lava was hundreds of years ago, before I was born."

They came to the end of the forest, and swooped sharply down the treeline toward the ground. Jill's stomach jumped into her throat and she let out a squeal that was a mix of fear and excitement. Just as quickly as she started to drop in the sky, Stelton started to climb again, centimeters away from touching the rock, climbing in the air along the rock formation until they were at the top. When they reached the tip of the volcano, they flew over the lip and dropped into the volcano's centre. Jill shrieked as she suddenly spun with the invisible creature who turned in circles in the air.

"Home sweet home!" Stelton shouted, then whooped out loud.

"You live here?" Jill asked.

"Yes we do. All of the survivors."

The inside of the volcano looked like a giant, empty salad bowl. A ledge portruded a few metres above the basin and ran around the entire bowl. Jill felt pressure against her waist again. She was lifted from where she sat and put down on the ledge.

"There you go. Safe and sound. Now that wasn't so bad, was it?" asked Stelton.

"Not at all, that was fantastic!" Jill said, clasping her hands together and pulling them under her chin. "Can we do that again sometime, Stelton?"

"I think we just might," he said. "Now, if you turn around, you'll find an opening in the volcano wall. Few, even among my people, know of its whereabouts. It's a secret passageway. Follow behind me. We'll follow this lava tube to the inner chamber. You've had an exciting afternoon. I imagine you will want nourishment and rest.

Chapter Fourteen

The passageway Jill entered was completely dark. The darkness reminded her of sleep, and in a strange way, she felt safe, invisible. The passageway was cool and the air in the volcanic vent helped to clear her head of the confusion from the last few hours. She felt disoriented and strange in a suddenly new and exotic world. In a strange way, it seemed as though the world's of the imaginary and the real were mixing together, at play, patched together, and for the first time in her life, Jill was suddenly aware that it was entirely possible that a thing could go unseen and yet still be real.

Jill was a very young girl when her mother died, and as she grew older, she often tried to remember her mother's face in her imagination. Jill could remember the colour of her mother's hair, a beautiful rich auburn, and she could remember the smell of her perfume, soft vanilla, a smell that reminded her of candlelight, but as hard as she tried, Jill could not remember the features of her mother's face.

Salma whispered a confession to Jill in Vendor that she had known Jill's mother when she was alive, *She had a beauty that would make a man's heart ache, one look at your mother,and he'd never forget her*. But even after she looked at pictures of her mother, when Jill closed her eyes, she could not remember her face. This always made Jill feel uneasy, even guilty, to the point that she started to wonder if she had any real memory of her mother at all. Perhaps the small flashbulb memories of her mother's hair colour and smell were things Jill imagined to fill the terrible void she felt at her absence.

Somehow, in this new world, in the darkness of the lava tube, Jill began to believe that all that guilt and doubt were the things that were least real. If she could speak to and fly with invisible creatures in an unfamiliar land, then perhaps she could one day remember her mother's face. The fact that the invisible creatures knew her mother made Jill burn with excitement, even desperation.

Jill waited for her eyes to adjust to the darkness in her new surroundings. After a few moments she was able to see the edges of the passageway walls. She stretched out her arm and put her hand against a wall. It was rough and warm to the touch, spotted with fingertip-sized holes.

"Just walk straight ahead," Jill heard Stelton's voice behind her. "The pathway is level. Soon it will be filled with light."

Jill started to walk slowly, tracing a hand along the wall. After ten or fifteen steps they came to a turn in the tunnel. From around the curve of the tunnel Jill could see the glow of torch light. Jill looked around in the dim light. The tunnel began to burrow downward further into the rock. The tunnel's ceiling was about a metre or so above her head and she could nearly touch both walls at the same time if she stretched out both arms.

"Wow," Jill whispered under her breath. "Where are we?"

"We're inside a lava tube that branches from the main vent at the center of the crater we just flew into," replied Stelton.

"Amazing! Where will it take us?"

"In a little while it will intersect with the main chamber where most of my people live. Far below the earth. But we won't stop until we reach the inner chamber."

"How far is it below ground?" Jill asked in wonder.

"Well, I'm not sure how far, but it goes directly into the magma chamber."

Jill stopped, puzzled. She looked in front of her at the spot in the air she imagined Stelton's face would be.

"The magma chamber is where lava collects below the earth before it spouts through the vent out of the volcano" Stelton said.

"Oh," said Jill, eyes wide. "Is it safe?"

Stelton laughed. "Don't worry Jill, we're safe. This is a dormant volcano. There hasn't been an eruption of lava for over a century."

Jill continued to walk the downward slope of
the lava tube. The further they walked the lighter
the passageway became, as more torches lit up the
way. They came to a place in the passage where
the ground no longer sloped but leveled out. At this
point the passage opened into a large cavern very
wide and high, and lit all around by large, flaming
torches. Jill looked up at the roof. From it dangled
massive spikes that looked like giant icicles made
out of rock.

"What are those?" Jill said pointing to the roof.
Her voice echoed throughout the cavern.

"Try to be quiet Jill, and do not step beyond
the shadows that shroud the edges of the chamber,"
Stelton said.

"I'm sorry," responded Jill.

"They are stalactites, or something very
similar," Stelton said. "Lava once dripped from the
holes in the vents above this chamber and hardened
into those formations. When I was young that was
one of my brother's favourite places to hide during
one of our silly games. One of the spikes is hollow
and there is a small hole through which he was once
able to crawl, when he was small, about your size. I
never found it; he showed it to me later in life, when
he could no longer fit inside. Take my hand, it is
important right now that no one sees you."

Jill felt Stelton grip her hand as he brought her
into the chamber. They walked against the walls in
the shadows where it would be difficult for Jill to be
seen. Finally, they rounded the curve of the chamber's wall and came to a very large opening. On

each side of the opening were three torches angled symetrically. The torches didn't touch the ground or the walls. Jill took a closer look and noticed that the torches did not hang from the roof either. She imagined it was some trick of the eye or some sort of magic that caused the torches to hang suspended in the air.

"Here we are, this is the entryway to the king's chamber. We will go there together," said Stelton.

Jill left the shadows and started to walk toward the entrance, but just as she was about to pass between the torches they quickly moved, crossing each other at forty-five degree angles in the path in front of her. Jill pulled her hands in front of her face to protect it from fire and took a quick step back. The other torches turned in the air at the same angle as the first set of torches, and completely blocked the entrance. All this happened very quickly, in a heartbeat, and as the torches moved, Jill heard loud, booming voices shout:

"Halt! Who goes there?"

Jill froze where she stood and looked beside her where she imagined Stelton stood. Even though she couldn't see him, since she entered the volcano, she had a constant sense of where he was. She found this interesting and strange, and wondered if it was the same sensation blind people had after they got comfortable with the furniture in a new room. Though they couldn't see it, with practice they knew it was there. The strange thing was that Jill could see everything, that is, everything but Stelton.

Jill heard Stelton's voice, calm and confident "This young girl is a friend."

"We have had no notice or order about visitors from the King. The human cannot pass."

"You have no order because the king did not know of the girl's arrival," Stelton said calmly. "But she can pass for she is welcome among us."

"Says who?" replied a voice that Jill thought had a smirk in it.

"Says Stelton Grey Wing, son of Eckwith, King of the Drylings and true prince of all the land of Acchora."

With that Jill heard the sound of metal sliding against metal. Suddenly, between the second and third set of torches a great metal sword appeared in mid air. It was nearly as long as the torches, as tall as a grown man. The blade of the sword shone in the firelight. The hilt was inlaid with red stones that glowed in the torch-lit darkness. The sword hung in the air, sword-tip pointing straight toward the stalactites Jill earlier admired. Almost as quickly as the sword appeared, did the torches move quickly back to their original positions; they no longer blocked the path. Two other swords, silver blades shining in the torch light, yet not as big and threatening as Stelton's sword, were drawn and floated in mid air behind Jill.

"Who dares defy the word of our lord, the Prince Stelton," said a voice from the two swords behind Jill. "Who will interfere with the business of the Prince?"

"Sorry, my lord, we didn't know it was you. We could not see your bodyguard either."

"No apology is necessary, guard. You could not see me and you did not know me or the girl. You were doing your job. I will be sure to tell the king he is under the protection of good Drylings. Now I must ask for your silence in this matter. You six are the only other Drylings besides my two guards that know a human child is among us. That information must be kept a secret until the King decides what to do with it. Do I have your trust?"

"You do, my lord," was the immediate reply from the voices behind the torches.

"Good. Then you have mine. May you have long lives and bravely defend our land. Long live the King!"

"Long live the King!" the voices shouted back.

"Now, Jill, if you will follow me."

Jill looked at the torches and remained in the place she stood.

"You are free to pass, Jill, do not be afraid," Stelton said.

Jill blushed, bowed her head, and slowly walked between the torches. Stelton's sword, suspended in the air only moments ago in front of her now pointed toward the ground at an angle and moved beyond the threshold of the entrance where it stopped. The two swords that were behind her rested in similar positions.

Jill stopped beside the larger of the swords, under the great arch of stone above the entrance.

"Stelton?"

"Yes Jill."

"You're a prince?"

"I am."

"I'm sorry."

"For what?"

"If I knew you were a prince I –"

"Child, please. It is I who should apologize for the treatment you received at the hand of our guards. Forgive them. It has been a long time since we have had visitors of any kind. A long time, and they have forgotten how to treat a guest. Forgive them and think nothing of my title. It is humble and insignificant at most."

"Stelton? I can now see where you are because I can see your sword!"

"Yes Jill, you can. When we move about above ground we must be very careful.

We try not to be heard or seen. It is to our advantage that we remain unnamed, unseen, forgotten. But down here, where we are safe, we let our whereabouts be known. It makes life a lot easier."

"Can you see the other Drylings?"

"I cannot, but I can sense where they are even when they are undercover.

Intuition is what some call it. A skill I have learned and honed over many years. However, no one is perfectly accurate when they use their intuition. That is why we show ourselves in the caves. It saves us from unnecessary bumps and bruises. I am older, and of the kingly line. The Guardian has blessed me with strong intuition. Sometimes another Dryling can sneak up beside me like I did to those guards, but that is very rare."

"You mean, they didn't know you were there either?" Jill asked.

"Not until I drew my sword. It takes someone of great cunning and strong intution to achieve such a feat."

"How do you know where other Drylings are when you leave the caves."

"That my dear child is a secret I cannot tell. A secret few others know. If the Dark Prince were to discover that secret, it might mean the end of our whole race. Only the King's most trusted officials know such a thing."

"Oh but Stelton, I would never tell," said Jill.

"I know child. You are trustworthy. But even that which you would swear to keep can be drawn from you through much pain. The Dark Prince would torture even a child your age in hopes of pulling from you our secret. You are trustworthy, but to save you from even the possibility of great pain, our secret I cannot tell. But you may know it one day."

"When? On what day?"

"On the day when all secrets are revealed and we, finally, are revealed ourselves.

But come now, child, enough talk. Let me bring you to the nest of my father! We must do so with much secrecy and speed. Cendol! Tickthith! Make sure the way is clear and see that the King is alone."

Jill saw the two swords rush away in front of her and quickly disappear. She stood in the dark corridor, alone with Stelton.

"Stelton?" Jill asked.

"Yes Jill."

"Who is the Guardian?"

Jill heard Stelton chuckle.

"I don't know that I can answer that."

"What do you mean. You said the Guardian blessed you with the ability to sense things."

"I did," Stelton replied.

"Then why do you say that you don't know him?" Jill asked.

"Because no one really knows the Guardian, Jill. He's very mysterious. The Guardian knows us, but we cannot know him, at least not yet."

Jill quietly thought about this.

"Is this one of his lands?" Jill asked.

Stelton did not respond.

"Stelton?"

Stelton's response was short and sad, a lonely violin: "It used to be."

After about five minutes of complete silence a sword appeared before Jill. She could hear the sound of laboured breathing.

"The corridor is clear my lord, you can have a private audience with the King."

Jill's hand was pulled to the hilt of Stelton's sword. When she gripped her hand around it her arm was pulled forward again. Stelton had started to walk at a quick pace through the stone corridor beyond the entrance. Jill had to nearly run to keep up. She held tightly to the sword.

"My father will be thrilled to see her," Stelton said.

"Just think, the daughter of Elizabeth Strong, here among us, all these years later," said the other voice, the voice of the returned bodyguard. "And at such a time as this!"

"Jill, your presence will greatly encourage my father and the rest of the Drylings.

Come!"

"But Stelton," Jill said, almost out of breath as she walked in hurried steps.

"What do I say to the King? What do I do?"

She had only just asked the question when they came to the end of the corridor and into another great chamber, a large oval shape, lit with ample torch light. Jill's breath stopped in her throat. The room was a sight to be seen. In the middle of the chamber was an enormous tree. High up in a large branch that thrust out of the tree toward the wall on Jill's right, was a great nest as large as an automobile. Jill had never seen such a tree before. The large leaves formed a canopy in the high branches that arched above the nest.

On the opposite wall, to Jill's left, a number of metres up, was a great hole in the rock from which cascaded a powerful waterfall. The water fell toward the floor of the chamber and collected in a steady stream which flowed toward the base of the tree then disappeared below the ground. From the foot of the tree, on a path that connected to the corridor from which Jill and Stelton had just emerged, were the same red stones that were set into the hilt of Stelton's sword. In the firelight shining from the torches along the chamber walls the stones glowed liquid red so that it appeared as though, when the water met the base of the tree, it was magically changed into a red stream of brilliant lava.

Jill stood in awe. She looked around the chamber and breathed in the sights. Finally, her eyes rested on the nest high up in the tree. In the middle of the nest, a large sceptre appeared. Though much larger and much more thick, the sceptre looked like the type of stick Jill might use on a hike through the woods. Yet, at the top of the stick was a large, transparent red stone cut into the shape of a flame of fire.

The sceptre suddenly dropped from the nest, and in the blink of an eye, towered directly above Jill. Jill looked up at the sceptre and gulped. The sceptre slowly angled toward Jill so that when it stopped, it was directly in front of her lips.

"Kiss the firestone, Jill," she heard Stelton say. "You have found favor with the King."

Jill leaned forward and hesitantly touched her lips to the stone. She expected it to be hot as fire. It was, however, cool to the touch. She gently kissed the firestone and then moved her head back. The sceptre returned to its towering position above her.

"Jill Strong, daughter of Grace, I present you to the kindness and favour of King Eckwith, Lord of the Drylings, rightful prince of all the land of Acchora."

Jill bowed her head and said, "Though I cannot see you, it is still an honour to stand in your presence, great King." The words were out of her mouth before she even thought about saying them. Jill quickly blushed and inwardly kicked herself. Then she heard the sound of laughter from Stelton and the King.

"It is I, Jill, who am honoured to stand, invisible though I may be, in the presence of one so great as you. Welcome to my humble court."

*   *   *

"You have come to our land in a desperate time," the King said to Jill. His voice sounded old but strong, comforting, wind blowing over tall grass. The King continued. "I am sorry we could not show you more courtesy, but instead had to smuggle you into my chamber with such secrecy. Your advent to Acchora would warrant great celebration any other time. However, for your sake, and the sake of the kingdom, it is best that your presence is not known at this hour."

"Why is it dangerous for my presence to be known?" Jill asked.

"For years, Jill, we have been fighting a silent war. Waiting, quietly, for our enemy to forget us. We have done all we could for over a century now, to slip from his memory. Waiting all the while for the right moment when his defenses are down and we can attack him openly."

"The Dark Prince?" Jill asked.

"Yes. He is a terrible enemy to my people. There is a history of great violence and hatred between us, though it was not always so. There was a time, when my people lived freely in Acchora, beyond the borders of the forest, near the water where we were close to our food supply. Those were the days before we retreated far back into the trees, before we lived in the caves of this volcano. There was a point in our history when the Dark Prince was our friend, or, so he wanted us to believe."

At this point the sceptre, which Jill presumed the King held firmly in his hand, tipped toward a spot on the ground beside the red stone path. Jill heard a sound like the snapping of fingers.

"Cendol, Tickthith. Find this girl a seat. Child, forgive me. Please, sit."

A round-shaped object floated from outside the chamber's entry way to the place the King's sceptre pointed to at the side the path. Jill thought it looked like a rather large coconut shell and noticed it was a sort of nest, though much smaller than the one like it perched up on the branch of the tree. Upon closer inspection, she saw that the nest was made out of brown sticks, mud, and soft leaves.

"This will have to do. It belongs to one of our hatchlings. Were you a Dryling, your age would be much too old for a nest like this, but it is just your size. I hope you find it comfortable."

Jill walked over and sat down in it somewhat hesitantly as if she was about to sit on a swing whose supports she was not sure would hold all her weight. Once she was confident it would hold her, she pulled in her legs and sat cross-legged in the middle of the nest. Jill imagined that she was a mother hen sitting on an egg, and nearly laughed out loud.

"It's wonderful. Thank you," she said. Jill cleared her throat and looked about the cave. She took a deep breath thinking, *What do you say to a King, and an invisible one at that?* "Uh," Jill started, happy to end the silence. "You said the Dark Prince was once a friend to the Drylings. How did he became such a terrible enemy?"

"I said the Dark Prince wanted us to believe he was a friend to my people. He never really was. His deception proved effective. So effective, he managed to enslave our entire race under a curse – a curse of great power that continues to effect our lives to this very day."

"What curse?" Jill asked, shifting in her seat. When the King said the word curse she felt a crawling feeling under her skin. She quickly looked over her shoulder.

"An evil curse full of malice, some of which your own dear mother helped us break free of."

"My mother?" Jill asked.

"It was not long ago that your mother stood in the very spot you now stand, Jill."

Jill looked around the room then down at her hands which she pulled into her lap.

"Your mother is a great hero in Acchora. When we heard of her untimely death, the kingdom grieved. Her loss is still felt. She will always be remembered as a woman of great courage and a

dear friend to my people. Why, she helped us find
our voices."

Jill sat in the nest still as a statue. She couldn't
explain why, but was suddenly overwhelmed with
the feeling that, no matter what, she did not want to
speak. She looked at her hands and slowly kneaded
her left index finger with her thumb. Finally, Jill
looked up at the King's sceptre and said, almost in a
whisper, "Can you tell me about her? Tell me what
she did here in Acchora?"

"Yes," was the King's response. "I do so gladly.
Your mother came to us during our most desperate
time in the history of our race. A time when we had
no voices, but could be seen. We had visible bodies
but no ability to speak. We were pitiable creatures,
crushed in spirit. The Dark Prince's evil nature had
only just been revealed to us. Suddenly we were
his slaves and to our regret and shame lived with
the fact that we had willingly chosen to enslave
ourselves to him, though we did so unintentionally.
You see, Jill, we had been a free race throughout all
our history. A kingdom undisturbed and untouched
with little contact with peoples or creatures from
other lands.

"All that changed when the Dark Prince came to
Acchora. In those days he was known to us as the
Rashtakar. He came to our King, my father, in peace
and a time of abundance. It was apparent he was a
creature of great wisdom and strength, deeply interested in our language, which he longed to study and
learn. He told my father that he traveled throughout
all known lands, seeking to learn and understand

new languages. He continually asked my father to teach him our stories and our songs, something my father was hesitant to do.

"You see, Jill, no one other than a Dryling had ever known our stories nor had any stranger learnt our songs. Our first story, our original story from which all other stories come from, ends with a warning to the keepers of language to protect our language as the great gift by which we as Drylings were meant to understand ourselves.

"Not long after the Rashtakar arrived in our land, a terrible drought struck Acchora. Suddenly my father was under much pressure from most other Drylings. There was little water to be found throughout our land. Fewer fish to eat; even the sea waters were barren. No one could explain the strange conditions we found ourselves in, even the highest order of Drylings could not understand what was wrong. Perhaps we had done some unknown thing to anger our Maker.

"It was in our growing hunger, confusion, and fear that the Rashtakar offered to channel abundant water from his land which would nourish the fish, trees, and bring other riches important to our livelihood. He said that if we did not, we would otherwise always be known in other lands as Drylings. It was the Rashtakar who gave us our name. Before he came to us, we were not known by any name.

"My father was a practical creature and he had a kingdom to think of. His people were starving. His people were thirsty. His people were dying. How could he know of the Rashtakar's intent? How could he know what evil would come of his decision? When my father asked what the Rashtakar would like in return for his great kindness, he asked only one thing, that the King would finally relent and give him lessons in our language.

"For the sake of all Drylings my father agreed. He taught our songs and stories to the Rashtakar in exchange for water and food. The Rashtakar told my father that the ruler of his land who watched our world had a secret magic that could ensure enough water could come from the Rashtakar's land to nourish our own. My father and his trusted advisors believed that the Rashtakar was an ambassador of mercy sent to us in our time of need. The Rashtakar was greater than any Dryling, and so it made sense to receive help from someone with more wisdom and power.

"At first the agreement was wonderful. Quickly after my father began to teach our language to the Rashtakar we had water and food again. Drylings were happy for being fed. But not long after, life as we knew it began to change. Until this point in our history, my people had never recorded our songs or stories in books. We remembered them. We never had need to write them down. We had thousands of stories and no books, such was our capacity to remember.

"It was only later that we discovered the Rashtakar secretly recorded each song and story he was taught by my father in a book. During the time period that my father taught our stories, we would learn of Drylings throughout our land who mysteriously lost their ability to speak. We were too slow to make the connection between the loss of speech and the teaching of our language. At first we thought there was a terrible epidemic throughout the land, a disease that was effecting speech. That mysterious disease was the Rashtakar's curse. With each song he recorded, more Drylings became voiceless. When my father finished singing our last known song to the Rashtakar, he lost his voice too."

As the King spoke, his voice grew quieter and quiter until he stopped speaking altogether. Jill patiently waited for him to continue. After a few minutes, the silence became awkward and she began to worry that somehow King Eckwith had also lost his ability to speak. Finally, to Jill's relief, the King continued:

"It still grieves my heart to think that my father sang his last song not to a beloved grandhatchling or to his Queen, but to an unknown enemy who meant to destroy his people's language and their way of life.

"When the words of the song were off his tongue, my father and all his court – I was with him in this chamber while he sang – realized what had been happening in Acchora. It was then the Dark Prince, for that is now how Rashtakar is now known among us, revealed his book. A large book that contained all our stories and songs which he closed and sealed with a lock. He stole our language from us and introduced my people to their darkest hour. Suddenly not one of us could talk. Not one of us could sing."

163

The chamber, once again, was silent for a very long time. Jill's heart gave a start when she heard the King's soft voice again, so intent had she been at imagining the tragic story in her mind.

"The Dark Prince soon enslaved us. He used our stolen language as a barganing tool to get from us what he wanted. In hopes that he would one day unlock his book and once again let us sing our songs, we were willing to do his bidding. He laid upon us a heavy yoke. Many of my people were taken from our land to his, and have never returned. Later, we learned it was the Dark Prince through cunning and cruelty who had dammed up our water supply and caused the drought. Somehow, he diverted fish from the sea coast. He made us desparate enough to wilfully give our stories away, something a Dryling King would never otherwise do.

"When we realized the Rashtakar's intent was always to steal that which was most precious to us, our spirits were crushed. Soon we learned how strong the Rashtakar's curse was: it was not only upon us, but upon our hatchlings as well. When the first voiceless Dryling was hatched and could not cry or make sound, panic spread throughout Acchora. My father never recovered from despair. He died in grief and guilt, feeling powerless to break his people from the curse and responsible for the terrible state of his people.

"The Drylings, however, loved him and saw him as a tragic figure who made a terrible mistake because of his love for them. When he died, there was open rebellion and war against the Dark Prince whose power was much greater than any of us perceived possible. His methods of warfare were cruel and brutal. We lost many, many lives. Too many to count. Too many to properly grieve. After the war, the Dark Prince left us for a long time, so humbled and worthless to him had we become. He told us he had other lands to visit, but that he would return. He left viscious brutes to rule over us in his stead. They still roam and ravage the land of Acchora."

The King's voice once again trailed off into a long silence. Jill's every sense was honed and tuned to the voice of the King. When he stopped speaking Jill realized she had been biting her nails the whole time he had been speaking. Jill put her hand in her lap. She waited for him to speak again.

The King sighed. "Your mother came to us during this time. If she had not come to Acchora, I believe there would be no more Drylings alive today."

"How did she get here?" Jill asked quietly, almost afraid she would ruin the near sacred solemnity of the moment.

"That is a mystery I've never solved, but I think she came the same way you came, from over the water."

"What did she do?"

"Your mother came with a book. It was a book that also had a lock on it, a lock without a key. Your mother was searching for the key with which to open the book that a great man had entrusted to her care. Somehow she stumbled into our land. And yet, though her arrival to Acchora seemed almost accidental, your mother was convinced that the timing of it was no coincidence. You see, though the the key was lost and she could not open the book, she could remember many of the stories in it.

"That is one way in which the Dark Prince's book was different from the one your mother had. When he wrote down our stories and songs, he not only stole our voices, but almost all memory of our language as well. Because we couldn't tell our stories, we slowly began to forget them.

"Your mother remembered many of the stories from the book, even though they were written down. She told us that she had been to other worlds whose inhabitants had similar stories to our own. Some were dying worlds whose inhabitants had given up the fight to find their voices. She told me she searched for the key to her book to ensure that her world would not forget its stories and die, and she challenged us to do the same. She was convinced that we were caught in the middle of a story, that better days would come but not without a price. She urged us to put down our swords and flee the rule of our enemy and his workers for a time. That's when we came to this volcano. We have lived here ever since. According to our time, that was more than two hundred years ago.

"Two hundred years?" Jill interupted, astonishment in her voice. "How can that be? My mother went in search of the key not more than seven years ago, when I was very young!"

"That is something we discovered when your mother was with us. Time in our lands is very different, at least, we record it differently. According to our count, it was hundreds of years ago, Jill. She came with us to these caves and lived with us until we could speak in her language."

"I don't understand. How could she? How could she communicate with you when she first arrived?"

"This is one of the greatest mysteries in our history. Even greater than how she arrived here at all. She said it was 'the Guardian's grace.' No one, not even your mother, knew for sure. When she spoke to us when she first came, it was in a language she had never heard, a language she had never learned to speak. And it was the same for us. We heard her speak a language we had never heard, or learned, but we could understand her as if it was our own language. Once we were in the caves, the new language we shared was gone. Our only conclusion is that it was some sort of magic, a Divine gift."

Jill saw the King's sceptre move toward her and felt his hand on her cheek. "All these years later, the daughter of Elizabeth Strong is with us. It almost pains me to see you, Jill, so similar in appearance are you to your mother."

Jill closed her eyes and tried to imagine her own face.

"Your mother came to us when I was newly crowned King. She was a great help to me. She saved me from the life of despair that was the tragic

fate of my father. She taught me new stories. Her
kindness will never be forgotten."

Jill heard the sadness and the love in the King's
voice and fought to hold back a tear. She bowed her
head, overwhelmed by what she heard. The King's
chamber was silent for awhile, except for the sound
of falling water. Jill felt her lips start to tremble.
She rarely spoke about personal things with others,
it wasn't safe to do so in Vendor, and when she did
her lips and mouth always tightened, a physical
reaction she could not control and always felt silly
about. Jill waited until she had composed herself,
until she was sure she could speak.

"Speak, child," said the King. "Whatever is
on your mind. Though I don't see it, I can feel the
heaviness of your heart."

Jill fixed her eyes on the chamber floor and
quickly said, as if she were speaking to the ground,
"I'm afraid I will sound foolish or selfish or both."

The King chuckled. "Speak your heart, child,
else silence make it a heavier weight to carry. And
later we will decide if you are selfish or foolish or
both."

Jill could feel King Eckwith's hand once again
under her chin. He gently lifted her face so that she
no longer looked at the ground.

"You do not have to look down, child. Look up.
Do not be afraid or ashamed."

"Your words, King Eckwith –" Jill stopped and
shook her head. "Your words about my mother
make me proud but they also make me feel so sad.
You speak of my mother's courage, the help she

gave to your people, her kindness. You speak these wonderful things that as her daughter I really want to hear. But at the same time, when I hear them, it is as though she suddenly becomes a stranger to me. Her face is even more of a mist, her voice –"

Jill bit her lip. When she composed herself she continued to speak. "I know she was kind, I know she loved me, but only from memory. They are memories that belong to a time before the time that you speak about. And you're right, it seems like a hundred years. They are the memories of a silly little girl. I hear your story about my mom and now I realize there is so much about her life that I don't know. Your memory of her changes my own and suddenly it feels like she no longer belongs to me. I feel like I've lost her all over again."

Jill sucked in a breath of air to stifle the sob that was about to burst from her chest.

"I'm sorry," Jill managed before the sob broke through and echoed throughout the chamber. Jill used her hands to cover the hot tears spilling down her face.

"Child, you have no reason for shame."

Jill heard these words from the King whispered softly in her ear and felt his strong arms embrace her. She felt softness like feathers completely surround her, but beneath the softness was a great strength. Jill couldn't remember the last time she had been hugged; the gesture of compassion comforted her and took away her embarassment, even the shame of her tears. How long she rested in those arms, she could not say. But she leaned fully

169

into their strength. Though, normally, she would have pulled herself quickly away from the embrace, Jill felt free and safe to remain in the generosity of the Dryling King's comfort.

When she opened her eyes, she found herself suspended in the air. But for the King's sceptre which lay on the ground and the swords of Stelton and his bodyguards, it looked to Jill as though she was all alone in the room.

"Memory is a strange thing, Jill," said the King who still held her in his strong arms. "But you must hold on to what you know. Your mother's love for you was real and still is real, though your experience of it may have changed for a time. For a little while you may not feel it, in the same way you, for a little while, cannot see us. But here we are. Your mother's love for you is as real as this embrace. How great your joy will be to see what for now you can only wait for, what you can only believe."

Chapter Fifteen

Jill couldn't remember a time in recent memory when she had felt so calm and secure as she did in those invisible arms. To Jill it was both wonderful and bittersweet to feel such strength and love and yet to be unable to see from whom these gifts of comfort were given. Jill was, however, unable to pursue these thoughts in more detail because Stelton's voice interupted her train of thought.

"Father, I imagine our young friend is quite hungry. I've been with her for the better part of the afternoon, and have not yet seen her eat. Before we discuss matters any further, why not let her have some food?"

"You're right, my son. Jill, are you hungry?"

Jill put her hands against her stomach. "I am now that you mention it."

"Then we will feed you with what food we have," said the King. "I hope you like fish."

"I love fish," Jill said happily.

"Please, you must want to freshen up. You are welcome to use my private chamber, there, behind the falls." The sceptre angled in the air and pointed toward the waterfall on the other side of the room.

"Make yourself at home Jill," said the King. "What is mine is yours."

"Thank you."

Jill walked toward the waterfall. When she got to the chamber wall, she realized that behind the cascading water was another room, much smaller than the King's chamber. Jill put her hand into the falls. The water was cold, mist from the falls collected in small jewel-like beads in her hair. Jill giggled and then stepped beside and behind the falls into the enclosed room.

"Jill —"

"Ahh!" Jill started at seeing Stelton's sword hanging in the air behind her.

"Stelton, I thought I was alone."

"Sorry Jill, I forget you can't sense me or the Drylings of my father's court. I'll close the door so you can have some privacy. It's too heavy for you to open or close on your own. Call when you're ready, and I'll let you out."

"Thanks, Stelton."

Jill stepped further inside the room. When the door was shut, the sound of the waterfall was muffled considerably. She looked around the room, which was lit all about with torches and something similar to a fireplace carved deeply into the wall opposite the entrance. The room was simple. Dryling furniture was all about, made out of leaves and sticks and mud just like the King's tree nest, although in various other shapes. It looked very neat and comfortable, and Jill thought twice about lying down on one of the nests and having a nap. Jill guessed it was the place where the King could have privacy and find sleep.

On one side of the room a rock much higher than Jill was tall, portruded from the wall for a few metres. It formed a right angle with, and extended until it nearly touched, the adjoining wall. Jill stepped through the small gap and found herself in another little chamber. Jill guessed that the entire room, including the small cordoned-off space, was likely carved into its present state from solid rock. Someone, likely a servant of the King, had carved the entire private chamber behind the waterfall!

Inside what Jill guessed was the King's private bathroom, water trickled down the outmost wall and collected in a small pool on the floor. The pool drained through a hole in the corner of the room. Opposite the water, on the other wall, was a large gem. It reminded Jill of the stones set in the pathway of the King's chamber, but it was a multi-faceted stone and of a slightly different colour. To Jill it looked like a large red ice sculpture of some abstract design with icicles pointing from the centre of the sculpture in every direction. Jill could see her reflection in the gemstone multiple times; when she looked into the stone she saw hundreds of little Jills smiling back at her.

Jill pulled her hair back and fixed it into a pony-tail and checked to see if she had anything unsightly stuck between her teeth. Jill stood with her face only centimetres from the mirror and examined herself. She tucked loose whisps of hair behind her ears, and for a moment searched for her mother's face. She remembered her mother was beautiful, something she did not see in her own face which she thought was more forgettable than anything else: lips she thought too pouty, high cheekbones that were quick to reveal shyness, dark eyes that matched the tone of her hair. She was just about to turn and freshen up by the water when the hair on the back of her neck stood straight up. Jill's muscles went tight. She could hear the sound of breathing very nearby. Deep, laboured breaths. Jill stood still and in a slow, cautious voice said, "Stelton? Is that you?"

The room was quiet except for the sound of the trickling water against the bathroom wall.

"Stelton?"

Jill looked at the opposite wall through the gemstone, but only saw empty space. What Jill heard next was so quiet and soft that she wasn't sure she heard it or thought it or if it had happened at all.

"He knows that you are here, and he will find you."

Jill turned quickly and looked to see who was behind her. No one. "Who's there?" she asked.

"He will find you." This time the voice was a little louder.

"Who? Who will find me?"

"You know him. The one who seeks you in your dreams."

"What does he want from me?" Jill asked in terror.

"The one who has been waiting, looking, wanting to find you. He is here."

"Where?" Jill cried.

"Here!"

At that, Jill turned and looked in the mirror, but she did not see her reflection any longer. Rather than hundreds of reflections of little Jills, there was one reflection of a beast, a large carnivore that looked like a bear, but was not a bear. It had dark lips and long white teeth that it flashed angrily. Jill screamed a horrifying scream and the image in the mirror quickly diappeared. When the image vanished, Jill once again could see her reflections: hundreds of little Jills that looked as though they had seen a ghost.

Jill thrust out her arm and tried to find where the voice had come from. She threw out her hands like a blind woman running through a thick forest trying to protect herself from unseen branches. She felt sudden pressure against her arm. Someone had grabbed her! Jill screamed again.

"Jill!" said the voice. Stelton's. "Jill, what's wrong?"

"Stelton? Is that you?" she asked.

"It is child. Are you alright? I heard you scream."

"Stelton, I don't think we're alone in this room. I heard a voice, I –"

Jill heard the metallic ring as Stelton withdrew his sword.

"What happened, Jill?"

"I saw something terrible in the mirror, then –"
Jill turned and pointed to the wall where the mirror
was. It was empty, a mere wall of stone. "I –" she
began, then stopped.

"What mirror Jill?" Stelton asked.

"It was there, on the wall."

"We no longer keep such things in our land, we
haven't for years."

Jill stood still in the middle of the room with a
blank look on her face.

"I don't know what happened in here. I was
frightened." She shook her head slowly. "Maybe it
was just a dream."

"A frightening one, by the sounds of it. I'm glad
you're alright," Stelton replied, softly.

Jill walked over to where the water trickled
down the stone, cupped the cool liquid in her hands
and splashed it in her face. Words she heard from a
kind, reassuring voice returned to her mind. *Do not
be afraid, Jill. Do not be afraid.* They were words
Seraph spoke to her in the Great Hall, many hours
earlier, words so real and ingrained in her memory
it was like she could hear them where she stood. Jill
massaged her temples and took a deep breath.

The image of the beast flashed again across her
mind and made her heart stop. She looked back
toward the wall where she had seen the mirror, but
neither it nor the beast were there. *Do not be afraid.*

Stelton's voice interupted Jill's train of thought:

"Come, Jill. Let me take your hand, let's eat."

Jill forced herself to walk out of the King's little bathroom at Stelton's pace which was much slower than she liked. When the door opened at the chamber's entrance, she felt a wave of relief. Jill could see a wall of falling water. The sound of the cascading falls reassured her and gave her strength. The door quietly closed behind her and Jill could not help but wish that it stayed that way for a very long time.

*　　*　　*

The food was delicious, just what Jill needed. Tempted to wolf it down in large bites, she had to consciously remind herself to eat slowly, like a lady in the presence of dignitaries. The stewards of the King had cooked a simple meal of fish with corriander seed, various herbs, and garlic, and it would have been perfect if Jill had some fresh butter to melt over the warm meat with a pinch of fresh lemon for good measure. Even so, Jill was happy with what she ate.

When she was finished with all the fish that she could eat, she sat back in the nest where she was served, and sighed deeply. She was served her food at the base of King Eckwith's great tree. The King did not say so, but it was clear to Jill that it was not appropriate for her to eat in the normal dining hall. The King and Stelton wanted to keep her presence a secret. Jill gave up wondering why, and decided to enjoy her food.

"That was delicious, just what I needed. What kind of fish was it? I don't think I've ever had it before."

"Sturgeon. A Dryling favourite" said Stelton.

"Oh, but not just any sturgeon, master," said a voice Jill had not yet heard, she guessed that it was one of Stelton's bodyguards.

"What do you mean?" Jill asked.

"Tickthith, maybe we should —" Stelton started to say, but Tickthith continued speaking before the prince could interupt him.

"When we caught the fish we found a rare seed in its mouth, silver in colour."

"A seed?" Jill asked, leaning toward the sound of the voice. "What did it look like?"

"Tickthith. I was hoping we could serve the child dessert and let her sleep before we talked about the seed." Stelton sounded frustrated, a tone Jill had not yet heard from him.

"Sorry, my lord."

"You found a silver *seed*?" Jill asked the question again. "Can you tell me what it looked like?"

There was a short pause. Jill heard Tickthith mutter under his breath.

"Never mind, Tickthith," said Stelton. "It was an honest oversight, I'm sure Jill is more interested in the seed than her dessert or even sleep. Tell her about it."

"My child, I have never seen a seed like it. It was much larger than any other seed I've seen. Though round it was much flatter, cold to the touch and heavy. And, like I said, it was silver in colour.

178

The fruit of such a seed must be a sight to see when planted in the ground. I wish I had more time to examine it."

"It has been a very strange day in Acchora, Jill" said another voice Jill had not yet heard. "Tickthith and I were fishing with our lord, prince Stelton. It fell upon us, as members of the King's guard, to catch the daily ration of food. No sooner had we started to fish then the strange spinning circle suddenly appeared on the harbor. Our lord the prince warned us to be alert but to continue to fish lest the Drylings under the King's care go hungry. Before the great wheel crashed into the sea, Tickthith caught this fish, the last catch of the day. We escaped to the forest just before that terrible wheel crashed into the water, surely deeds of the Dark Prince."

Jill cleared her throat and bit her lip. Cendol, the voice she was now able to identify as belonging to the other bodyguard of Stelton, said, "Go, on, tell her about it, Tickthith."

"This fish, the one we now speak of that you have since enjoyed as your meal, was large and awkward to carry, especially in my haste. It gave quite a fight, thrashing its body all about. As I flew toward the trees I dropped the fish onto the sand. When I swooped down to pick it up, I grabbed it by the neck, and the seed we spoke of fell from its mouth into my hand. I was examining the seed when the wheel hit the water. I'm ashamed to admit it, but the impact of the wheel with the water startled me, and I dropped both the fish and the seed. When my lord the prince called me to leave the beach, I grabbed the fish, but could not find the seed. We, all three, watched in awe to see two young children arrive in our land from over the water, then in great interest as you explored the beach, looking for what we now understand was your seed."

Jill tilted her head to the side and squinted her eyes, confused.

"Then which one of you three spoke to us on the beach?"

The room went absolutely silent.

"What do you mean, Jill?" asked Stelton.

"My friend Simon and I, we heard a voice on the beach. It was loud and frightening and sounded like it surrounded us, and was inside of us, and above us. It warned us to be careful, to be careful what our little eyes would see. It was the last thing we heard before the strong wind buried the object that you call a seed. That was before Simon was pulled under the sand." Jill closed her eyes and thought about Simon.

"Jill, are you saying that someone else saw you?" Stelton asked. "Someone else spoke to you on the beach?"

"I guess so."

"You guess so, or you know so?"

"I – I'm not –" Jill stammered.

"I'm sorry to be so insistent, Jill," said Stelton, "but it is crucial for us to know if you spoke with someone else today."

Jill fought back tears. "I'm not sure."

"Jill you need to be sure, this information is crucial to the safety of the Drylings!" Stelton said.

"I don't know!" Jill nearly shouted. "I'm sorry, I just really don't know. What is real and what is not real? What is a voice, what is a dream? One moment I was in my world, exploring in the Great Hall, and the next moment I entered yours. Ever since I've been in Acchora I've been hearing voices belonging to creatures I can't see. What is my imagination and what is not? I don't know. It's starting to drive me crazy."

Jill paused and collected herself. If she had a twig in her hand she would have snapped it. She wiped at a tear that started to fall down her cheek.

"Stelton, the girl is tired," interjected the King. "She's had a long day. Let her sleep. If someone saw the girl, there is nothing we can do about it. Jill, we will talk more of this in the morning."

Jill wondered, even though she was tired, if she would be able to sleep at all. As she was led toward the place she was to spend the night, she imagined she was a prisoner on the way to trial. She could not shake the thought that Simon heard a voice on the beach too. If somehow her life depended on it, she would say *someone spoke to us, a warning, and then the wind blew.*

Chapter Sixteen

W hen Jill closed her eyes it was to images of a terrified Simon sinking into the sand, or of terrible white teeth behind black lips. Jill was tired but could not sleep. Stelton had brought her to a nest high in the branches of King Eckwith's tree, nearly but not quite out of earshot from the King's own nest where Stelton and the King spoke in hushed tones. Jill would have preferred sleeping snugly on the ground, but suspected the Drylings were more comfortable to know she was safe and sound high in the tree where she could not easily be detected, a place she could leave only with the help of one of her new, invisible friends.

Through a crack in the side of the nest, Jill could see the swords of Cendol and Tickthith at the entrance to the chamber, guarding the door lest anyone come in and disturb the King. As she was told, Jill stayed out of sight and was careful to remain below the high edge of the nest in case another Dryling entered the chamber and happened to see her. Jill lay flat on her stomach against the bottom of the nest, like a soldier ducking in a trench, and strained to listen in on the conversation between the King and his prince. If she controlled her breathing, she could make out most of what the two said.

"… but we cannot stay in such a state of secrecy much longer, son, the Drylings will start to get suspicious. The last time the King's chamber was closed was –"

"I know, I know," interupted Stelton. "When your father was on his deathbead."

"The people will start to worry. They will at least expect one of the healers to give a report of my condition. We've already told a lie to them that I am not in good health. Not even family is allowed in the chamber. Surely our families will start to suspect something peculiar is happening."

"I'm afraid that is already the case," Stelton replied matter-of-factly.

"What do you mean, son?"

"The voice the child heard. Father, you know it could be none other than –"

"No. I won't believe it."

"But father –"

"Do not mention his name. Do not break my heart. I could not endure it."

Jill leaned forward into the nest's wall when she could no longer hear any voices. She propped herself up on her elbows and pressed her ear into the soft wall. After long minutes of silence, her arms started to ache under the weight of her upper body.

She was about to shift to a more comfortable position but kept dead still when she heard the voices of father and son again.

"There are already a growing number of Drylings who question –" Stelton's voice dropped to a whisper. Jill nearly pushed her head through the nest's muddy wall to hear what he said, "– who question why we still walk invisible in our world. Many call her strategy a curse. The story is being remembered differently, it is changing. If these Drylings find that the daughter of Elizabeth Strong has come over the waters –" Stelton stopped. "I fear for her life. I also fear for your kingdom, Father. You may have a revolt on your hands. If he knows there are human children in Acchora, if he discovers who the children are, the next Drylings who come through the chamber's door might very well come with swords demanding to know why we harbour a sorceress!"

Jill shivered. *A sorceress?*

"Such Drylings are absurd!" King Eckwith's voice raised above a whisper. "They've forgotten what it was like to have no voice. They forget the indignity of the curse. They are few in number, son. They are a minority."

"Ah, let them come then!" Stelton said. "I welcome their swords. I will teach them a much needed lesson."

"Things could change quickly, that's one lesson we have learned from the past" replied the King. "Our way of life is soon coming to an end. Change is inevitable. It has been for a long time. Jill's arrival marks it, son. *The* change we have waited for since the fateful day Elizabeth gave us our voices."

"I believe it father. And I believe that her daughter will help us find our place again in this world."

"May it be, may it be."

"And what of the boy-child?" asked Stelton.

"Her friend's arrival to the land is unexpected. Never before has a human boy-child set foot in Acchora. Nor has anything from another world ever been planted in our soil. Whatever he planted grew very quickly. Some sort of creature that pulled him into the ground. I pray that it did not pull the boy to his grave, I have so long wished to meet one of his kind."

"He would not come all this way only to die. The Guardian would not allow such a thing," said Stelton. "If he is alive, he is deep below the earth where no Dryling has ever traveled before."

"May the Guardian give him courage and strength," said the King. "My son, I agree with you, we must keep silent about the girl still a little longer. It may very well be that her presence on this island is already known and that even now our home where we have hidden ourselves for so long is under threat of conflict we as a race have not known for a very long time. But these things are out of our control. If they are true, we must wait for the confrontation and hope we have the strength to endure the storm."

"Let our foes reveal themselves; then we shall reveal our strength to them. Long live my father the

King. May the blood of your enemies spill by the wrath of your sword."

*　　*　　*

Jill woke in pain. She had fallen asleep with her arms under her chest. When she tried to move them they felt like heavy cement blocks, and they tingled with pain, the same way her feet felt, thawing after skating on a frozen lake in the winter. Jill had slept against the edge of the nest. She sat up and noticed two bowls in the middle of it, one filled with water, the other with what looked like bird seed.

Jill slowly peered over the edge of the nest down toward the King's perch in the tree. She saw no sceptre or sword. There was no sign of the invisible Drylings at all. Jill looked over at the food and frowned.

"I'm hungry, but not that hungry," she said aloud.

Jill heard the sound of laughter. "Good morning Jill, you slept long and hard. You were tired. How do you feel?"

Jill looked around the nest, but saw no sign of Stelton.

"Good morning Stelton. Now, it's really not fair. I have no way of knowing where you are unless you show your sword."

"I know that, Jill, I'm sorry," said Stelton. "I was trying to see if you would be able to sense me, I wanted to test whether or not you could intuitively sense my presence."

"Is that possible?" asked Jill.

"To learn to sense and listen to what you cannot see? Of course it is. How do you think I learned?"

"I thought you were maybe born with it, you know, that it was something special to the Drylings."

"We've had a long time to learn it," said Stelton, "but it did not come naturally to us. Our disappearance, our invisibilty forced us to learn and get better at it. Still, many Drylings refuse to learn, they have not adjusted to our new way of life."

"But that won't matter, will it Stelton, once you are returned to your original selves and you get your bodies back."

"I don't know, Jill. Perhaps then we will have ears to hear other things in the world that cannot be seen."

"Like what?" Jill asked.

"Like messengers from the Guardian. Your mother says they fill the world."

"Really! What sort of things do they say?"

Stelton chuckled. "That, my dear child, I have yet to discover. My father knows. He has heard such messengers before."

"What did they tell him?" Jill asked.

"I don't know," replied the Dryling.

"What do you mean you don't know?"

"My father won't tell me. He said I must wait for my own time. But I can tell you what I think it is like. I think they are mysteries, secret and magical. Beautiful things no Dryling mind could ever make up. My hope is that when my hearing is sharp enough, they will retell me the original stories of my people, the ones that were important to us but were stolen and lost. Our first stories."

"I hope you hear them some day, Stelton, I really do. How will you learn, though, if no one tells you how to listen?"

"Well, I didn't say that," Stelton said. "No, my father has taught me how to listen. He says that when the messages come, you can know because you can feel it. Your heart quickens, or maybe your breath stops. You will be busy with the every day things of life and suddenly you'll feel a presence."

"Do they speak, um, do they speak out loud to you?" Jill asked.

"Not necessarily. My father says it's like you suddenly know something that you didn't before, somewhere between your imagination and your heart, it's so real that you feel you hear it, but not with your ears. It's the same way you know someone is behind you in the dark. Before you turn around to look, you know someone is there. My father says the trick is not to turn and look, but to wait. Don't try to see, or the moment will pass."

"I don't like the idea of someone I can't see sneaking up to me in the dark," Jill said. "Stelton?" she started to ask, then stopped.

"What is it, Jill?" he asked.

"Nothing. It's just that, I understand what your father means. I've had these sensations before. I've had them as recently as last night."

"What do you mean?"

"That feeling that something is really happening, that someone is really speaking, and that it is something you imagine, but also something very real." Jill closed her eyes, then looked at the red stones in Stelton's sword. "Stelton, are any of the Guardian's messengers – I mean, is it possible that some of his messengers are *bad*?"

"From the Guardian? No. That's impossible."

"Well, then can any other sort of creature communicate in the same way as his messengers?"

"I've never thought of that," said Stelton. "But, I guess it's possible. I should ask my father. Why, Jill? What have you heard?"

"Last night, when I was in the king's inner chamber, when I screamed and you came to me. After hearing you speak about listening to invisible things, I'm starting to realize that I wasn't having a bad dream. In fact, now that I think about it, I think I've heard such messages, good and bad, for a very long time. Even in Vendor. I just didn't know that they could be anything other than my imagination."

"What did you hear yesterday, Jill?" Stelton asked.

"That's the thing, Stelton. It wasn't just something that I heard. I saw something too. It was so real."

"What was it Jill, what did you see?"

"I heard a voice, and I saw a terrible creature. One I fear that has been following me for a very long time."

"What did the voice sound like?" Stelton asked, urgency in his voice.

"It sounded like your voices. I know it was not the King, and I know it was not you, Stelton. But I've only just heard Cendol and Tickthith speak, however I don't think it was them."

"Cendol, Tickthith," Stelton shouted, "come here at once."

Within a matter of seconds, Jill saw the swords of the two Drylings appear and hover near Stelton over the nest.

"Cendol, where were you last night when Jill was retired to the King's private chamber?"

"When you sent the human child to refresh herself in the King's private chamber I was sent to the kitchen to fetch the child's food," replied the bodyguard.

"Tickthith?" asked Stelton.

"I was with Cendol, sir, as you ordered. We don't normally serve food, but under the circumstances, you decided it best that no one else enter the King's chamber."

"Jill," Stelton asked, "was it the same voice you heard on the beach?"

"I don't know. I really don't. It could have been. It wasn't a voice I was familiar with."

"What did the voice say?"

"It said –" Jill closed her eyes to think. "It said that he knows I am here. The voice said that he had found me."

"Who?"

"I don't know."

"Cendol, Tickthith, go summon my father from his private chamber. Wake him if he sleeps. It may not be safe for him to be alone in there. We must meet with him at once."

The two swords dropped out of sight and glided above ground toward the waterfall where they disappeard.

"Jill, you must tell me what you saw," Stelton said when the two guards left.

"I saw a strange orange stone. It was like a mirror, it was in a strange shape, the shape a school child in my world would draw a sun. It reflected many images of myself at first when I looked into it."

"A gemstone!" Stelton whispered.

The swords of Tickthith and Cendol reappeared, accompianied by King Eckwith's enormous sceptre.

"Good morning, Jill. Son, you have an urgent message for me?"

"Father, Jill has found a gemstone."

"Where?" asked the King.

'In your private chamber," Jill said. "On the bathroom wall. At first I thought I dreamed or imagined it, because when Stelton came into the chamber to find me, it was no longer there."

"I have no mirror in my private chamber. There is nothing on any of my walls.

Since the wartimes it has been an edict that no Dryling can adorn their walls with any picture or any mirror. It is to protect us. To protect us from –"

The King stopped mid-sentence. "Son, what other news do you have to share. I can sense the urgency of your heart."

Stelton recounted his conversation with Jill to his father, from the moment she awoke. "Jill, you said you saw a creature in the mirror," said the King after Stelton had finished his report. "What did he look like?"

"He was terrible, frightening. He was a beast. He looked like a bear, or a wolf, or a wolverine – he wasn't any of those things alone. He was all three at once. He had a terrible black mouth, and razor sharp teeth. And I think the voice I heard was right in what it said. I have seen him before in my dreams."

"He is here, then," King Eckwith said.

Jill heard the sound of metal against metal as all four Drylings drew their swords.

"The Dark Prince?" Jill whispered under her breath.

"Yes," replied Stelton. "Rashtakar, the Dark Prince."

"Guards, enter my chamber and look for the gemstone. If you find it, destroy it if you can, if it is not too late."

Jill saw the swords of Cendol and Tickthith glide toward the King's private chamber and disappear behind the waterfall again.

"How is this possible?" Jill asked. "How did he get here? I thought the Dark Prince couldn't find you, that he had forgotten you!"

"It was our great hope," said Stelton. "But our fears have been confirmed. We have a betrayer among us. For some time we have had reason to believe that someone very dear to the King's family, someone the King once believed dead, still lives, and now plots against the King."

"Who?" Jill asked.

"Someone with power enough to slip past our senses and reach the King. My brother," Stelton said. It sounded to Jill as though he had the wind knocked out of him.

"Your brother?"

"Oh Stelton, I'm so sorry. I should have told you what I saw yesterday when it first happened," said Jill.

"It's okay, Jill, you didn't know."

"I thought it was my overactive imagination. It's Ms. Steinbeck – she's convinced me that I have an annoying habit of imagining unreal things."

"I wish you were imagining things. But I'm afraid you were not. I think we are both learning that you do have an incredible gift for intuition."

"Jill, do you have any idea why the Dark Prince is following you?" The King asked.

"I think I have something that he wants, something entrusted to me. Seeds, like the one Simon planted into the ground."

"I see," King Eckwith said. "I see. Stelton, we must warn the people. Send the Drylings guarding the entrance to my chamber throughout the mountain. Tell the people to retreat deeply inside its caverns. Tell them to bring what food and water they have. Tell them to be silent, to hide. Tell them the Rashtakar has found us and that they need to be ready to fight. Equally ready to flee. Hurry!"

Stelton's sword dropped out of sight.

193

"King Eckwith," Jill said. "It's me who the Dark Prince wants."

"He wants my people too. He has waited and searched, for years he has looked for us. Somehow he has found us. We will do what we can to protect you, Jill. Fear not. Come, take my hand. We must hide you while there is still time, among the stalactites."

The King took Jill by the hand and pulled her into his arms. They dropped from the top of the tree to the ground. Air rushed past Jill's face. She was happy she had not eaten any breakfast when the King set her on the ground.

As Stelton returned, from across the chamber, they heard the sound of laughter. Jill saw the swords belonging to Cendol and Tickthith fly from the waterfall and crash onto the ground only a short distance in front of her. Cendol and Tickthith moaned in pain. The swords quickly returned to the air, swordtips pointing toward the ceiling.

"Fly King Eckwith! Fly!" Jill heard Tickthith shout.

"Tickthith, you're injured!" shouted Stelton who returned to the base of the tree.

Jill looked and saw a thick yellow substance flowing from a spot in the air a few centimetres above the upturned hilt of Tickthith's sword.

"Take the child and fly. Both of you! Fly!" shouted Cendol. "We will do what we can to defend you and to hold off Kelton as long as we can."

"Then it is him!" said the King. "How do you know?"

"He spoke with us, from the gemstone that hung in your private chamber just as Jill said. We were unable to remove it. He fought us with great force. He is stronger than he was before. He has more power, more skill. He is dangerous."

"What has happened to him?" asked the King, to no one in particular. "Never has a Dryling drawn the blood of another Dryling. It cannot be!"

"Father, it is the Rashtakar's influence" said Stelton. He has changed him."

"I will stay!" said the King. "I must speak with my son."

"King you must fly!"

Suddenly a different voice began to speak. A voice Jill recognized: the voice from behind the waterfall! The voice from the beach. It was similar to Stelton's voice, only higher in pitch. It made Jill shiver.

"Since when does a subject command a king? Much has changed in this land since I left it, father."

"Kelton?"

"Yes, it is me. Your son, back from the dead."

Kelton laughed. His voice came from all directions. Jill turned to the right and to the left, spun on her heel and looked behind her.

"We mourned your death, Kelton. Every Dryling that survived the cruelty of the Dark Prince," said Stelton.

"You mean every coward that left the war; every traitor that abandonned the fight and escaped to this mountain under the magic of that witch who you call a saint."

"She saved us, Kelton. She gave us a new language to speak," said King Eckwith.

"Saved us, ha! You speak, but you cannot be seen. You cannot be seen so you cannot truly live. You are fools!"

"Show yourself, Kelton, let us see your sword."

"Oh, I will show you more than my sword. Father, here is your son, returned to you from the dead."

A sword suddenly appeared, it's tip at Jill's throat.

"Kelton, you will not harm the girl," said Stelton, frantically.

"Oh, I know, brother. I have orders. She will not be harmed. She has something of great value that my lord the King wants."

"Your lord the King?" asked Stelton. "There is only one king in Acchora, brother!"

Jill stood totally still, holding her breath, trying not to move in order to keep the sharp sword from cutting into her skin. Jill felt a strong arm around her shoulder, and heard Stelton's voice behind her assure her that he would let no harm come to her.

"No harm will come to her if she gives me what I seek," said Kelton.

Out of the corner of her eye Jill saw a sword flash toward her, and the sound of a very angry cry. The sword at her throat quickly pulled away just in time to clash with the other.

The swords swung in dangerous and terrible arcs. Each time the metal hit metal, large orange sparks burst into the air, lighting up the chamber.

Suddenly, a sword fell to the ground and Jill heard Cendol cry 'Mercy!' Just as suddenly the other sword arced toward the sound of Cendol's voice and struck a terrible blow. The moment Jill heard the sword make contact with Cendol's body, she suddenly saw him, a great majestic creature with enormous wings that filled the air in front of her. The wings dropped suddenly to the ground, and the creature collapsed. Human-like hands clutched around the hilt of the sword that pierced his torso. As suddenly as Cendol cried in pain and appeared before her, he fell limply to the ground, dead.

"Cendol!" shouted Stelton.

Before Stelton could move to help his fallen friend, the sword that impaled Cendol was pulled swiftly from his stomach.

"Father," said Kelton, "behold your son."

With that, Kelton suddenly appeared before them. Like Cendol he was huge and majestic, but terrifying. He stood in front of Jill, sword lifted above his head by human-like arms, strong and bulging with muscle. From the shoulders burst enormous wings that were extended outward in their full span. The wings reminded Jill of a bat's that, when stretched, were almost transparent in the light. His chest, torso and legs were covered in light brown feathers, and he stood on strong leathery feet that had very sharp talons. Kelton had a short thick neck with a head shaped like an eagle's, but with an almost human nose and mouth where there would normally be a sharp, curving beak. His eyes were most astonishing. Intelligent eyes that, when fixed on Jill, seemed to see every one of her insecurities and pierce her soul as sharply as the sword that he pulled from Cendol's fallen body. When he looked at her, Jill felt exposed.

"My son!" the King exclaimed. Whether King Eckwith spoke in anguish or with awe, Jill could not tell. "My son, what have you done?"

"I have become myself, again, father. I have been made whole."

"Whole?"

"Yes. I've been restored to my body. I've been restored to my true self."

"Your true self? Look at you."

"Aren't I wonderful, father?"

"I see no more compassion in your eyes. You have changed."

"I am better. I am greater. My lord, the true King, will empower you also, if only you will stop resisting him, hiding from him. Submit to his good leadership, father, and he will make you whole also."

"Good leadership?" Stelton interjected. "Submit to him? So what, Kelton, so we can become murderers like you? Submit to him so he can teach us what? To betray our people?"

"Murder, betrayal. These are things I know nothing about, brother. They are your methods of warfare. I desire to restore us to our original state. No, better! I desire to bring our people to a place far beyond what we have ever been."

"And what is that, Kelton?" asked King Eckwith. "What is that?"

"Our true selves. You know, father. To have that which all these years we have longed for. To return *home*. To be wholly seen and wholly heard again. To know our history again. To have our stories back. To sing our songs again. The true King has promised me that he will make it happen."

"What will it take for you to see his promises are lies, Kelton?" asked King Eckwith.

"But you don't understand. He will give us our stories back. We only must be patient for a little longer. We need only wait, submit to him, and he will make good his promise."

"When Kelton?" asked the King. "When?"

"There are many other lands beyond our own. Many other people. When the true King has recorded their languages, when he can speak them all. That is when he will give our stories back to us. He longs to know all languages, and for all stories to belong to him. He only wants to become like us so that we can become like him."

"How quickly you have forgotten our tragic history, brother," said Stelton. "Don't you see that you are deceived? I don't know what dark magic he has used on you, but it has clouded your mind. The Dark Prince, for that is your King's real name, will ruin every other land just as he has ruined our own. He doesn't want our language, he only wants to steal it from us so that we forget who we are and become his slaves. That is who he really is. A cruel leader. A tyrant. He cannot accept that the Guardian made other peoples far different, far greater than him, and so he will stop at nothing to ruin them.

We do wait, patiently, for the day when we are no longer separated from our language and our bodies, and on that day we will sing again. But it will not come by submitting to your false king."

"Then how will it come?" asked Kelton who pointed his sword toward Stelton and squinted his eyes.

"It will come by killing him," Stelton said.

"Careful, brother, my loyalty to the true King is unmatched," said Kelton. "I will strike with my sword again."

"You would kill your own brother?" King Eckwith asked, his voice a whisper.

"And receive much honour and power when I spill his blood. But I have not come for you, Stelton. I have come for the girl."

Jill stepped backward into Stelton who still stood behind her.

"You cannot have her," Stelton said.

"Do you really defend the daughter of that witch? She is the very reason you are in your miserable state."

"What?" Jill asked.

"Has he not told you, girl? Your mother, before she left this miserable land, after she taught King Eckwith this silly, stuttering, language of yours, used some dark magic against the Drylings and made them disappear."

"What do you mean?" Jill said, angrily.

"Your mother sang a song the night she left Acchora, and when that song was finished, the Drylings could no longer be seen. She pretended to be a friend. But she turned out to be a formidible foe. Not only did she replace the Dryling's language with something as debase and uninspiring as the language they now speak, but she separated them from their bodies. When she abandonned them, she left them with nothing but a foreign tongue, and she made sure they would never again be seen."

Chapter Seventeen

Jill was stunned. Was what Kelton said true? If so,
how come Stelton or the King had not told her
so? Jill's cheeks went hot with anger.

"Stelton, is what he says true?" asked Jill.

"Not the way he describes it, Jill, it was
different than that," replied Stelton, calmly.

"Different?" Kelton asked. "There is no other
truth than this, girl-child: your mother was a liar
and a sorceress. She did more harm among this
people than she did good. The sooner you accept
that, the better. Now, give me what I came for. The
Rashtakar doesn't care whether you live or die. All
he wants is the treasure you carry with you. It is
very valuable to him. If you give it willingly, you
might save a life or two."

Jill clutched her hand around the coin pouch's
drawstring that hung from her neck, under her shirt.
"Then you came for the treasure given to me in the
Forest?" Jill gasped. "How do you know about it?"

"How else do you think it arrived in this world but that my lord wanted it to come here?" asked Kelton, his lips curled in a smile. "I had hoped to avoid this unpleasant family renuion by taking it from you on the beach, but I was prevented by a strong easterly wind."

"I will never give up the treasure," Jill said, hands clutching tightly to the coin purse. "It is mine to keep."

"Maybe I can persuade you otherwise," said Kelton, and he snapped his fingers.

When he snapped his fingers, Kelton turned and looked behind him at the waterfall. Another creature, identical to Kelton, though smaller in size, appeared. In front of him, wearing brown corduroy pants, white sneakers, and a blue T-shirt was a young boy with orange hair and green eyes.

"Simon!" Jill shouted and tried to run toward him, but Stelton's strong hands on her shoulders stopped her from advancing toward him. "Simon, are you alright?"

"Never been better," Simon said.

"Silence, boy!" shouted Kelton.

The Dryling walked with a firm hand on Simon's shoulder to where Kelton stood. Simon smiled at Jill, then quickly said, "Don't listen to him, Jill, no matter what he says! He's afraid. You —"

But Simon couldn't finish. Kelton stepped toward him and struck him on the face with the back of his hand.

"I said be quiet!" Kelton shouted.

"Kelton?" King Eckwith said to the other Dryling that stood behind Simon holding the boy by the shoulders. "Kelton, is that you?"

The Dryling looked quickly in the direction of King Eckwith's voice. "Father?"

"Silence, fool!" shouted the Dryling holding the sword to Jill, and struck creature on the mouth. "You also are not to speak."

"Kelton, is that you my son?"

"Yes father, responded the Dryling. Father, I hear your voice."

The King pointed his sceptre to the impostor Dryling who was pretending to be his son and commanded: "Show yourself Rashtakar! End your trickery!"

Suddenly the creature that stood before Jill, sword drawn, screamed loudly. He drew his wings in front of his face. When he withdrew them he had completely changed in apperance. Standing before her, now, was the image Jill saw earlier in the gemstone mirror. A large, towering beast of a creature with dark brown fur. He was large as a Kodiak bear and had a face that looked both like a wolf and a wolverine. The creature had terrible yellow eyes that were blood-red at the center, thin black lips, and sharp fangs. As he thrust his wings behind him, they morphed into a dark black cape.

"So we meet again at last," said King Eckwith, calmly. "You have as many appearances as you have names, Rashtakar. I could sense the evil in you. No son of mine could be so ruthless and sinister."

"Nor as shrewd and powerful," replied the Rashtakar.

"What is your purpose?" asked Stelton.

"What other than to demand your allegiance and to take back what is rightfully mine?" the Rashtakar said as he looked down at Jill, smiled and licked his lips.

"You have no claim to the treasure. It belongs to the Guardian and always will," Jill said.

"You cannot resist me child. You will not. Nor will any of your friends. If they do, you know what will happen."

The Dark Prince looked over at Cendol's fallen body.

"We will fight you to the death," said King Eckwith as he raised his sword.

"No you won't. You will hand the girl over to me willingly."

"And why would I do that?" asked the King.

"Because I hold hundreds of your people – people who, like the son you once thought was dead, are imprisoned below the very land you call Acchora. One foolish move, and with a word, I will order their execution. And you, like your father before you, will be responsible for the deaths of many relatives, subjects, and friends."

King Eckwith's sword faltered. "I do not believe you," he said, his voice choking. "We would sense their presence, we would intuitively know they were alive. Ever since Elizabeth Strong sang her song and we disappeared, though we could not be seen, our other senses have developed. Ever since the

Final Disappearing we have grown in our ability to sense the unseen!"

"Not when they live thousands of feet beneath earth and rock, cut off from even your ability to sense and communicate, great King. Tell him, Kelton. Is it true?"

The real Kelton bowed his head and spoke to the ground. His shoulders weighed by the burden of his words. "Father, what the Rashtakar says is true."

"It can't be!"

The Dark Prince pulled an orange stone from under his cloak and showed it to King Eckwith, it was similar to the gemstone Jill had earlier seen on the wall, only much smaller. The Dark Prince snapped his fingers and instantly, the image of many terrible creatures appeared in the flat surface of the stone. They stood in a large chamber, their bodies bent and crooked. They had terrible yellow eyes and sharp white fangs and held weapons in their claws. Behind them were hundreds of Drylings, fully visible like Kelton, crouched or sitting on the ground.

"And you, little girl," continued the Rashtakar. "You will not resist me, for if you do, your young friend will die, right before your eyes. He will die and you will be responsible."

"Simon!"

"Jill," Simon cried, "don't listen to him, please!"

The Dark Prince struck Simon on the face once again. Simon fell to the ground.

"Kelton, do something!" shouted King Eckwith from where he stood.

"Father, I can't, his power over me is too great."

The Dark Prince stood over Simon and raised his sword, tip toward the ground. He held the hilt high above his head, ready to thrust it through Simon where he lay on the ground.

"It is your decision, Jill. The treasure, or your friend. What will it be?"

Jill grabbed the coin bag from around her neck. "No treasure is worth the life of a friend. You can have it. But, I will only give it to you once Simon stands beside me, and Kelton too. You must agree to leave us in peace. Or else you will have to pry this treasure from my hands."

Jill said these words with such boldness, that she surprised herself and every one else in the room. The Dark Prince, also to her surprise, quickly lowered his sword. He took one step away from Jill as though he had been hit by an invisible force. He staggered for a moment where he stood and then started to laugh.

"Jill Strong, you are as arrogant and as foolish as your mother! But, have it your way." The Dark Prince prodded Simon in the ribs with his clawed foot and told him to stand beside Jill. Kelton slowly followed.

"Now the treasure, hand it over."

Jill looked at the treasure and then at the Dark Prince. She hesitated for a moment until the Dark Prince raised his sword.

"Keeper, forgive me," she said, then threw the pouch of coins at him, just beyond his reach.

The Dark Prince, realizing the treasure would hit the floor, lunged for it, but could not catch it. The orange and white bag hit the ground and the contents of the bag spilled out. Instead of nine silver coins, which Jill expected to see, there were nine seeds that bounced all about the rock floor.

"What is this?" shouted the Dark Prince. "What have you done with the treasure?"

"Nothing!" Jill shouted back in disbelief. "Nothing, I promise!"

"You *promise*? This is not the treasure! What did you do with it, you lying little witch? Where have you hidden it?"

"I have done nothing. I haven't looked at the treasure since I entered Acchora."

Jill looked at the seeds that were on the floor. On several of them she could see small green and white buds sprouting from them since they hit the ground only moments before.

"If you will not tell me where the real treasure is, your friend will surely die."

Jill screamed as the Dark Prince lunged toward Simon with his sword. Simon was frozen where he stood, unable to move. Just as the sword was about to penetrate his chest, Kelton threw himself into Simon, knocking him off his feet. Kelton's reaction was quick, but not quick enough. The sword meant for Simon penetrated his body under his left wing.

The Dark Prince screamed an angry, violent scream.

"Tickthith," shouted Stelton, "take Jill and the boy. Fly! We will fend the Rashtakar as long as we can."

The two invisible princes, King Eckwith and his son, attacked the Dark Prince. Their swords flashed in the torchlight and sent the beast backward. Jill felt a hand around her arm as her feet started to leave the ground. Simon was off the ground too. Jill squirmed and kicked and got free of Tickthith's grip.

"Jill!"

"Tickthith, you must leave me. Take Simon, he doesn't know the way. I'll be right behind you. I must collect the seeds. I was commanded to protect this treasure no matter what."

"I can't do that, Jill, I've been ordered by Prince Stelton."

"And I've been ordered by someone as great as he to keep the treasure at all costs. Please, Tickthith, you have to let go of me."

Jill felt Tickthith's grip on her arm release.

"Thank you."

Jill ran toward the seeds and started to pick them up. The buds were longer now, some nearly as long as she was tall. Jill scooped up the seeds one after the other and dropped them into the pouch. She counted eight. *Where was the ninth?*

Jill quickly scanned the room. Somehow, one seed found it's way to the base of King Eckwith's tree in the centre of the chamber. She looked over to where the Rashtakar fought with the two Drylings. She could see that the Drylings were injured.

Yellow blood gushed from various places in the air. The Dark Prince, however, was wounded too, and fully engaged in battle.

Jill ran and grabbed hold of the ninth seed, whose buds were already burrowing into the soil at the base of the tree. Jill had to pull at the seed to get it free from the ground. After a few tugs, she was finally successful.

"Aha! Got you," she said, pleased with herself.

"Those were my thoughts exactly."

Jill quickly turned around. She looked up into the terrible face of the Dark Prince. He towered over her and sneered, sword in his hand. Though he towered over her, he was not as tall as before. He was injured, bent at the waist and breathing heavily.

"You should have run when you had the chance, Jill. But now I will have to kill you. Just like I killed your mother."

"*You* killed my mother?" Jill said, as her face drained of blood.

"It was one of the greatest of all my feats in the lands beyond the Forest."

"You evil, evil creature," Jill muttered.

"You want to know what her final words were, before I slit her throat?"

Jill closed her eyes tightly.

"She said, 'you can kill my body, but you cannot have my soul.'" The beast laughed wickedly. "Do you believe that, Jill?"

Jill was silent. The Dark Prince pushed her against the trunk of the tree.

"Do you believe that, Jill?"

Spittle shot from the Dark Prince's mouth and covered her face. She could feel his hot breath against her skin. "Here we are again Jill, but this is no dream. Do you believe what your mother said?"

Tears filled Jill's eyes. "I don't know." Jill fell to her knees on the ground.

"Oh, come now Jill, stand up. At least die with dignity."

Jill bent over the ground hardly able to think, her mind a blur of rage and fear.

"I said get up!"

Jill looked at the evil creature and set her jaw. She quickly grabbed some dirt in her hands and shot up from the ground throwing the dirt into his eyes. The Dark Prince let out a shout and stumbled backward, swiping at his face. Jill kicked him as hard as she could in the knee, hearing it crack as she forced it to bend the opposite direction. She did not wait to assess the damage she had done to his body, but ran toward the exit of the King's chamber instead. She was nearly there when she felt sharp claws gouge into her back. The Dark Prince had recovered and caught her in his cruel grip. He turned her around and pushed her against the chamber wall, her face very near to the burning flame of a torch.

"This is where it ends for you Jill. Your short life is finished. You were doomed to failure; doomed to death by my sword."

As the Dark Prince raised the weapon above his head, Jill in one desperate motion, grabbed the handle of the torch and pulled it from the wall, swiping the flame across his face. The beast let out a terrible scream. The fur on his face caught fire. He frantically clawed at the wound to put out the flame, spinning around wildly, but his face continued to burn. Finally, he ran over to the waterfall and threw himself into the water. His body disappeared from sight. After a few moments, the beast's head emerged from the falls. His voice was weak and shrill. He looked directly at Jill with his blood-centred yellow eyes, then pulled his face back so that only his mouth could be seen.

"I will find you," said the thin black lips. "I will hunt you. I will follow you in your dreams. When I regain my strength, then will I find you Jill Strong, and we will finish this!"

With those words, the mouth opened wide and let out an angry, horrendous scream of rage. The Dark Prince completely disappeared behind the waterfall, and did not return.

Jill leaned against the wall, stunned by what events had passed, hardly believing she was still alive. Then, she looked over toward the tree with a start. She could make out two very faint shapes leaning over the fallen Kelton. As Jill approached the figures, she realized that she was looking at a barely visible Prince Stelton and King Eckwith. Their forms could hardly be seen against the back-drop of the chamber walls. But Jill could see faint traces of their feathered bodies, and stately eagle-like heads.

Kelton was coughing, and breathing irregularly. "Father," he said, "I am so sorry! This is all my fault. For years the Dark Prince has persecuted us far below the earth, and for years we have attempted different escapes. When I finally broke free from the deep darkness, I could sense you were alive." Kelton tried to sit up from the position where his father held him in his arms.

"Don't move, son," said King Eckwith. "Reserve all your strength."

Kelton leaned his head back into his father's arms and continued, his words slower and said with much pain. "My joy was soon crushed when I realized my escape was only part of the Dark Prince's plan to use my intuition to locate you and your perch. He used the same cruel threat against me that he used against you – the death of our people should I resist him. I am ashamed to say that I was not as brave as you, father. I was unable to resist him. I became his unwilling servant, though it was for the love of our people." Kelton gasped for air and held his hands over his wound.

"Son, don't despair. You are forgiven. You do not die in shame, but with honour. And now when I die it will also be in peace, knowing my beloved son maintained his integrity. A son returned to me from death, after all these years. Son, do not fear."

Tears welled in Jill's eyes as Kelton's body relaxed and he breathed his final breath. Jill stood there silently crying as she watched King Eckwith, with Stelton, stand over his dead son. It was some time before either moved, the sound of the waterfall the only sound in the room.

The King walked over to Jill and put his hand on her cheek. Jill could see the features of his face, but even as she looked at him, she could see through him to the chamber walls behind. King Eckwith carried strength and dignity in his face. His nose was a sharp line, noble, his mouth kind. Even in grief it looked as though he smiled. His eyes were gold like the sun, and when she looked into them she felt as though he could read her thoughts and felt as though she would like very, very much, to know his.

"Child," he said. "Thank you for your tears."

Jill smiled weakly and held the King's wrist between both her hands.

"King Eckwith, I can see you."

"It is just as your mother said, child. The Dark Prince is losing his power."

Chapter Eighteen

"Simon!" Jill shouted as she ran over to him and gave him a hug. "I thought I would never see you again."

"She refused to let us bandage her wounds until she knew that you were alright," said King Eckwith to Simon.

Simon held out his hand which had blood on it from Jill's back. "Jill, you're hurt!"

"The wounds aren't that deep. You took a few blows too," Jill said, pointing to the blood on his face.

"The Dark Prince?" Simon asked, looking beyond Jill and the two Drylings that had walked with her up the lava tube into the enormous magma chamber.

"He's gone, at least for now," Jill replied.

Jill, Stelton, and King Eckwith had walked slowly from the King's chamber, each through the lava vent to the magma chamber where Jill had earlier encountered the King's guards. Tickthith, now also slightly visible, had hidden Simon in a hollow stalactite high in the ceiling of the cavern.

It took Jill and Simon some time to notice that they were being watched by hundreds of eyes, kind and inquisitive. Partly-visible Drylings hovered in the air all around them, emerging from vent openings all throughout the chamber. The creatures quietly stared at the children. Both Jill and Simon blushed and smiled, sheepishly raised their hands to the creatures and waved.

"Drylings of Acchora, draw near," said King Eckwith, standing behind Jill and Simon. "Today, great and terrible things have happened among us. The Dark Prince has been in our midst and nearly took my life."

The crowd gasped.

"You have lost one of your greatest sons, Kelton Strongwing son of Eckwith, who died in an act of bravery to save the lives of not only this young boy-child, but many of your fellow Drylings, imprisoned far below us, beyond earth and stone."

The gathered crowd began to look at each other and whisper, the warm, energetic sounds of an orchestra warming up before the conductor walks on stage.

"And, to our humble race has come a great friend and ally who has helped us realize our long awaited desire to be made whole again. Drylings of Acchora, it is my honour to introduce you to Jill Strong, child of Grace who came to us over the sea, as did her beloved mother, Elizabeth Strong."

A wave of surprise washed over the crowd. There was a moment of stunned silence, then one Dryling fell to his knees. After him others followed, old Drylings and young, wives and hatchlings, all bowed to their knees and pointed their wings in the air.

"Drylings of Acchora, remember this day. For it is a great day, the beginning of a new era, the first taste of our long awaited hope." When the King had finished speaking, he bent and kissed Jill on the cheek. Jill looked into his peaceful eyes and smiled.

"King Eckwith!" Jill cried, as he collapsed to the ground. Jill turned and knelt over him.

"King Eckwith, are you alright?" Simon asked, joining Jill at the Dryling King's side.

"I'm fine, children. I'm fine. I've never been happier."

"But you look hurt," Jill said.

"To think, in my day, I should see the beginning of the restoration of my race.

My father dreamed of this day, but I see it."

Many in the surrounding crowd rushed to the King's side. Two guards cut through the crowd, gently lifted him off the ground and carried him out of the room. Others, including Stelton, came to Jill. Many wanted only to touch her. Some held her hand, others cupped her face in their hands, or kissed her on the cheek. Jill felt strangely comforted by each word of thanks, each touch of compassion, each mention of her mother's name. And the whole while she was enamored with the depth and humility behind each set of Dryling eyes.

217

Stelton stood beside Jill the whole while, and finally addressed the crowd. "My friends, there will be time and place to give our regards to Jill and to Simon.

There will be much celebration in the days and weeks to come. But our young friend was hurt by the Dark Prince, and her wounds must be attended to. And, I expect, she is in need of some much deserved rest."

The crowd of Drylings started to step back, a few straggled and walked with her toward the entrance that led to the King's inner chamber. Simon, Stelton and Jill were greeted by small groups of shy but kind Drylings. As Jill turned to leave, she felt a hand around her wrist. Jill turned, smiling, to say goodbye to the Dryling, but the Dryling did not smile back. Instead he squinted his eyes and frowned. He looked older than most other Drylings: his grey feathers were not as dark or firm. His eyes were not as bright, and were covered by thick, bushy brows. He seemed to look further into her than the others did, beyond her, through her.

"For giving us back part of ourselves, I give you my thanks, Jill Strong. But do not be fooled by the outpouring of gratitude you see in this crowd today. You will be watched; you will be evaluated. The royal family too quickly allows outsiders into its confidence. There are other Drylings who are not so rash. We refuse to be ruined again by another race. We will stop at nothing to make sure the past does not repeat itself."

Jill stood still. The Dryling stooped to speak to her, his face was very near hers, she could feel his warm breath on her face. Jill all of a sudden felt tired and weak. She wondered what to say, her mind was completely blank.

"Olmander, I see that you have met the child," said Stelton, who managed to pull away from a group of Drylings.

"Yes, we've met. I was just thanking her for – for, helping us," the Dryling said and smiled curtly. "And I was just going to tell her how very much she looks like her mother." Olmander stood to his full height and crossed his arms across his chest. "The resemblence is striking, almost disturbing."

"Yes, I too see traces of Elizabeth in her face," Stelton replied, putting his hand on Jill's shoulder. "Let's go now Jill. I will take you to one of our healers. You need rest. Good day, Olmander."

The old Dryling nodded his head. Jill could feel his eyes follow her all the way to the entrance to the King's inner chamber. As Jill, Simon, and Stelton crossed the threshold to walk down the slanted corridor toward the Royal chamber, Jill stole one last glance at the old Dryling. He remained fixed where he stood, his piercing eyes watching her as she moved, arms across his chest, a frown cut across his lips.

*   *   *

Stewards of the King separated Jill and Simon from each other. These Drylings attended to the children's wounds, gently cleaning their cuts and then applying a dark mud-like substance over their injuries, Jill's on her back, and for Simon on his cheek and lip where he had been hit by the Dark Prince. Once their wounds were cleaned and dressed, and they had been given a drink that was warm and sweet to taste, they were able to speak with each other.

"Well, Jill, it looks like you've had a far more interesting go at things than me.

You're a great hero. You fought the Dark Prince. You're the friend of a King!"

"All in a day's work," Jill smiled and rolled her eyes. "I feel like I've landed in a strange dream and can't wake up." Jill slapped Simon's back. "And what about you, Simon? I want to hear about your adventures below the sand. I'm so sorry — I tried to reach you, or at least join you, but by the time I jumped, the sinkhole was closed. What happened?"

"It was terrible, Jill. You know what it's like to have sand in your swimsuit? This was way worse. I swallowed nearly half the beach, and the whole time I was clutched in the grip of those terrible arms. If his arms didn't crush me, I thought the sand would suffocate me. Either way I thought I was dead."

"What happened?"

"Have you ever felt things were so dark and hopeless, and then in the next instance, everything has changed? In the blink of an eye, in the next breath. I thought I was in the grip of death, but then realized I was very, very wrong."

Jill started to laugh.

"What?" Simon asked. "Now what are you laughing at?"

Jill kept laughing so hard, sound no longer came out of her mouth.

"Jill, you're scaring me? What's got into you? I'm serious here."

Jill ran her hands through her hair and took a deep breath. She wiped a tear from her eye. "I know Simon. I know you're serious. The answer is yes, it's just that, if you had asked the same question of me a few days ago, I wouldn't have understood what you mean as well as I do now."

Simon looked at Jill, closed one eye and squinted with the other. "The last few days have been crazy," he finally said. "When we were on the beach –"

"Children!" Stelton called, gliding up to Jill and Simon. His right wing had bandages on it, and he had some of the dark mud salve on his face and chest. "Sorry to interrupt, but I have an urgent request. A member of the King's guard has found the gemstone in the King's private chamber. The Rashtakar left it in his haste. We believe we can follow him into his underworld. Simon, now that my brother lies dead and the Dark Prince has fled, you are the only person who knows the whereabouts of those Drylings so long imprisoned. We fear they are in danger. Perhaps the Dark Prince and his evil workers have left Acchora, but we fear that in his flight he will harm our people who are trapped under the ground. We know it has been a long and excruciating day for you, young Simon, but will you go with me and a group of the King's guard and help us find our friends?"

Simon looked at Jill and then at Stelton. Jill smiled uncomfortably.

"It may be dangerous Simon," Stelton continued, "we might encounter the Dark Prince again, but my father wills that we risk danger if only to save our people."

"I'll go with you," said Simon, quietly.

"But Simon, you just got back. You're injured," Jill said.

"Sorry Jill, you'll have to talk later, we have no time," Stelton said drawing a small dagger from under his wing and handing it to Simon. A number of Drylings glided over to where they stood. One of them put his hand on Stelton's shoulder.

"Master, we must leave, we cannot delay another moment."

"I'm coming with you," Jill said, standing up and following behind them as they whisked away.

"No Jill," Stelton said as he stopped and faced her. "You cannot come with us.

Your life is too valuable."

"Too valuable? And what about Simon's?"

Simon stopped and looked up at Stelton. Stelton bowed his head and looked at the ground.

"His is of great value too, Jill. But he can go where you cannot. He knows the way into the Dark Prince's evil underworld. You must stay above ground, here, with my father. He needs you at his side, his life is slowly fading away. He will give you instructions about what to do if we do not return. I can say no more, dear child. We must go."

Stelton bent down and kissed Jill lightly on the forehead. "Continue to be brave, Jill, continue to be strong."

And with that, he turned. Simon looked at Jill and smiled. His eyes looked sad and tired, but also full of adventure. "We will meet again, Jill, I'm sure of it," said Simon. "We have both faced death and adventure before, and look at us," he shrugged his shoulders, "we're still alive."

"We are still alive," Jill repeated.

"Simon!" Stelton called from where he stood at the waterfall watching the two children. The other Drylings had already disappeared behind the falls.

Simon turned and ran over to the waterfall.

"Simon?" Jill shouted.

Simon stopped and looked back at Jill. She raised her arm in the air and waved.

"Be careful, Simon!" she shouted. "Be brave!"

Simon nodded his head and raised his dagger into the air, then disappeared behind the waterfall. Jill watched the water cascade from the rock into the pool below. She felt numb. She was overwhelmed. So many thoughts and emotions competed for her attention, but she was nearly too tired to think. And Simon. She had so many questions to ask him. Questions that would have to wait, as her friend encountered the uncertainty and danger of the new adventure he now pursued.

A hand touched Jill's arm. "Jill? The King
would like to see you." It was a voice she had not
yet heard. A female Dryling's voice. Soft, but firm.

"Where is he?" Jill asked the Dryling.

"He is reclining in his perch. I will carry you to
him."

"Is he alright?" Jill asked.

"For now, yes," said the Dryling. "Only time
will tell."

Jill nodded her head. The Dryling scooped her
up in her hands and pushed off the ground. In a few
flaps of her wings, they arrived at the tree in the
centre of the chamber. The King's nest was a large
oval shape that was rasied in the middle. Jill thought
it looked like a very large sombrero, although with
much higher brims. The King was not perched
in the centre of the nest, but leaned with his back
against the mound where he normally sat. His wings
covered his torso. He looked very comfortable and
relaxed, but from his face, Jill could see he was in
pain. The Dryling set Jill down in front of the King
and flew up high in the tree where she perched on
a branch. King Eckwith kept his eyes closed as he
addressed Jill.

"Have they gone, then, Jill?"

"Yes, King Eckwith. Stelton and Tickthith, and
the others, and Simon with them."

"He's a brave boy."

"He is. Will they be alright?"

"I don't know Jill," said the King.

"Could I not go with them?"

King Eckwith opened his eyes and looked at Jill. "You are needed here." The King grabbed his side and grimaced in pain "Don't you see that Jill?" he asked. "You've done so much for my people already, in a single day. Will you stay a little longer with us? Will you help us Jill?"

"What do you want me to do?" Jill asked, unable to imagine what the King had in mind.

"I need you to help my people believe."

Jill turned away from the King and leaned into the edge of the nest. She rested her chin on her hands and looked out over the chamber below. The King stood up, staggered toward Jill, and leaned against the nest beside her. She turned and looked into his astonishing eyes. Jill searched his face and frowned.

"What do your people need help to believe?"

"What they already are starting to see: that they can once again be free. We must take dominion, again, of Acchora, and so undo the work of the Dark Prince. But first," the King said turning to look out over his chamber, and sweeping his arm dramatically from where he stood, "first we must leave all of this."

"Leave the mountain?" Jill asked.

"We cannot hide any longer, Jill. We must leave."

"Do you think the other Drylings will agree with you? Will the others leave?"

King Eckwith bent down and began to dig away at the mound of dirt at the base of his nest. After a few moments of digging he pulled a small red stone from the dried mud. He stood slowly and then held the stone out for Jill to see.

"They will have to," said King Eckwith. "They will have no choice."

Jill looked at the small stone. It was the same colour and shape as the ones below the tree forming the lava-like path. "What is it?" she asked.

"It is the plan that will save my people from their lives of fear and drudgery. Tell no one of it, my child. It is our secret for now. We must wait until the time is right."

King Eckwith dropped his hand to his side, then let out a long sigh. Jill pursed her lips, and nodded her head. The King returned the stone to its place in the mound and covered it once again with dirt. He then returned to the edge of the nest and leaned against it.

Jill stood beside the King and looked across the chamber. She watched water from the falls surge from it's height then splash onto the chamber floor. Jill quietly imagined the thoughts of King Eckwith, then quietly tried to understand her own. She felt like a single drop of water, thrown into the air by some great force, exhilarated by the power of flight, but also anxious about what it would be like to make impact with the ground.

Chapter Nineteen

*D*own, *down, down*. Simon could still hear the words. *Further, deeper. Below rock, and time, and sound*. The voice terrified him more than the strong hands that clutched his body in a tight grip. The words frightened him more than his fear of death when he was pulled from the beach through the sand. Simon shook his head, hardly able to believe that he was retracing his steps, a single glowing rock lighting the dark, as he went in search of the creature belonging to that voice.

*   *   *

When Simon jumped behind the waterfall, he entered the King's inner chamber. Seven Drylings, members of the King's guard along with Prince Stelton, stood in the room. Two of the guards held the multifaceted orange gemstone, one side of the mirror was cracked.

"Can it still be used?" asked one of the guards holding the gemstone.

"I don't know," Stelton said. "Simon, where was the gemstone when you entered the room?"

"It was on the other side of the dividing wall, across from the wall of falling water."

"That's where Jill said she saw it."

"Jill knew about the gemstone?" asked Tickthith.

"She saw it when she was alone in here the other day. She had some sort of encounter with the Dark Prince. He was watching her through the gemstone. When she screamed I ran in to help her, but the mirror was gone. We both assumed it was a dream."

"How did it disappear?" Tickthith asked.

"I think my brother was in the room. He hid the mirror and himself from me. He was always good at hiding. How terrible it would have been for him to stand in here, finally returned to his beloved country, yet held hostage by the Rashtakar's evil threat against our imprisoned brothers."

Stelton walked over to the gemstone and took it from the two guards. "I've never seen a gemstone like this," he said. "My people have never used one to enter another world. Do you know how it was used, Simon?"

"The Dark Prince showed me how to use it, I had to enter it on my own to get to Acchora."

"Can you show us?"

"I hope I can. May I?" Simon took the stone from Stelton's hand and walked over to the wall of water. He put the gemstone in the falling water and let it pour over the stone.

"In a few moments the mirror will reflect light. It gets really bright so you may want to cover your eyes. Once the the mirror glows, we can put it against the wall."

Simon's prediction was right. After the gemstone soaked in the water it started to glow with unnatural light so that when Simon pulled the gemstone away from the water, it looked like he held a miniature orange star in his hands. The boy placed it on an outcropping rock that formed a shelf along the opposite wall.

"Now what?" asked Tickthith.

"If you breathe against the central piece of round glass, the stone will fog up, then you must say the name of the place you want to go. When I ended up in this chamber, I said "Acchora," into the glass, then put my hand into the fog, and the next thing I knew, I was here. Your brother told me the name of the land where the other Drylings were imprisoned. The name is Melchura."

"What did it feel like?" asked Tickthith.

"Moving from Melchura to Acchora? It's hard to describe, but it was very strange. It hurt as much as when the Dark Prince hit me in the face, but in a different way." Simon rubbed the back of his neck, remembering the pain. "Who wants to go first?"

"I will," Stelton said, as he stepped toward the gemstone.

"No, my lord," said Tickthith, "let me go. Perhaps foul creatures wait our arrival on the other side. I cannot let you go first."

Tickthith stepped up to the gemstone and breathed on the central piece of glass-like stone. The centre fogged and the Dryling's reflection was no longer visible in the middle. Tickthith turned to Simon who nodded his head in assurance. The prince's guard leaned toward the stone and said "Melchura." Instantly, the fog on the stone's surface formed a cloud that left the mirror and swirled in the air. Tickthith stepped back and watched the cloud. It slowly emerged from the mirror, growing bigger and bigger until it was the height of his body. Tickthith pulled his sword from the sheath under his wing and extended his other hand into the fog. In the next instant, he was gone.

Simon blinked. The fog started to turn in the opposite direction, shrink, then pulled back into the mirror. Stelton walked up to the gemstone and saw his face reflected in the middle stone. He leaned into the stone and breathed. Once again his image clouded up with fog. As the cloud of fog started to turn and emerge from the mirror, Stelton turned to Simon and lifted him so he could speak into the mirror.

"Simon, why don't you go next. I'll quickly follow."

As Simon said the word "Melchura" into the stone, a huge flame burst from the edge where the mirror had cracked. Stetlon and Simon fell onto the ground.

"Prince Stelton, look!" Simon shouted. "The cloud is starting to pull back already. The gemstone is broken. I think this might be the last chance for anyone to go through."

Even as the words were coming out of his mouth, Stelton unsheathed his sword, grabbed Simon and ran toward the cloud, which had shrunk to the same height as Simon was tall. Stelton dove forward into the cloud like a circus tiger through a fiery hoop, leaving the other Drylings behind in the King's chamber.

Simon felt a rush of air, and just like his passage into Acchora, his entire body went rigid and tight, as though he was being pulled and stretched from all sides, pressure that, anywhere else, would split skin and cause bones to crack. Simon could hear Stelton yell in pain, then realized he too was screaming at the top of his lungs, pushed forward with the speed of a freight train, and at the same time falling downward from a very far height. Try as he could, he was unable to move his arms in an attempt to break his fall, he could only imagine what it would be like to suddenly hit the ground. The thought terrified him.

And then, just as suddenly as Stelton grabbed him and jumped into the foggy portal, the momentum and pain stopped. There was no impact against the ground, no more pain or movement. It took Simon a moment to realize this was so. Simon stopped yelling. He opened his eyes and looked all about. He was in a very dark space. Behind him a circle of flame burnt on the wall.

"Simon, are you alright?"

It was Stelton's voice. Simon squinted his eyes and could make out Stelton's faint form next to him in the dark. He was sitting on the ground, his shoulder the height of Simon's head. Simon looked up into Stelton's astounding eyes. They were brown and gold, with emerald green flecks that glowed in the darkness. And yet Simon could see the dark rock through the eyes; the Drylings were still only partially visible.

"Yeah, I'm okay."

"That was quite the sensation," said Tickthith, "fine by me if we take another route back to Acchora."

"It looks like we'll have to," Stelton said, pointing at the flame on the wall. "The path we took into Melchura has been destroyed."

Simon realized that the existing light they had would soon burn out, the flame on the wall was already dwindling. "Hurry!" he said, "we have to find something that will burn, to keep the fire. It's really dark down here. If we want to find our way, it will be easier with light."

"Can the boy-child not see in the dark?" Tickthith asked his master.

Simon stopped scanning the darkness, looking for a stick or piece of wood that could substitute as a torch. "You can see in the dark?" Simon asked.

"The prince could find his way through here with his eyes closed," Tickthith said, "such is his ability to see."

"We're able to project sound off of solid objects in front of us in the dark, that way we can see without using our eyes. These stone walls are fine walls to bounce sound off of," Stelton said. "We've become accustomed to it, living underground for so many years. But Tickthith exaggerates. This way of seeing is much more limited than he'd like you to think."

"Can I hear it, your sound?" Simon asked.

"If you haven't yet heard it already, you will not hear it at all. I make the sound even now."

Simon strained to hear the noise, but heard nothing.

"You can't hear it with your ears, child, the sound is too small for humans to hear. There is some sort of path over there," Stelton gestured to Simon's right. "I cannot hear where it ends."

Simon looked puzzled, he squinted his eyes and looked for the path. As he did, the remaining flames marking the portal through which they entered Melchura flickered out. Their surroundings went completely black.

"Not again," Simon moaned. "I hate the dark."

"Don't worry, Simon," said Stelton.

Simon felt something weighty and cold in his hand.

"I brought something from our world. It will help you to see."

Simon looked down at the rock Stelton placed in his hand. It was red in colour and glowed like the 'exit' lights above door frames at the movie theatre in Vendor. Simon held it up in the air; he could see Stelton at his side and Tickthith who stood an arm's length from his master, but not much further beyond.

"Thank you Stelton, what is it?" Simon asked.

"We call it a 'lava rock.'"

"It's amazing. How long will it last like this?"

"Hopefully long enough for us to find the lost Drylings and bring them home. It will keep its light for many days. But I hope to find the Drylings sooner than that."

"That would be very nice," Simon whispered.

Stelton turned and looked at the path. Simon walked past the Drylings and started to follow the path downward.

"We may as well start moving," he said. "It's a long way down to your friends."

"Simon, you must be careful! The Rashtakar might be on the loose down here. He won't be happy to see us. We must be on our guard."

"I'd be willing to bet this lava rock that we won't run into him," said Simon, who kept walking. "He hates it down here. I heard him say so. And now that he's injured, I think he'll go far away, somewhere to be alone, away from your friends. He hates being around them too."

"Why do you say that?" asked Tickthith.

"Because there are so many of them. Your brother said he's tried many different ways to get rid of all the Drylings he imprisoned, but every time he tries, his plans fail, and they grow in number. Even as prisoners and slaves."

"How many Drylings did you see down here?" Tickthith asked.

"Only a few hundred, but I think there are many more."

"Hundreds of Dryling?" Stelton asked. "How can it be?"

"It's amazing what can happen when you plant something in the ground."

Stelton looked at Simon and furrowed his brow.

"That was something your brother said."

Stelton chuckled. "That sounds like something Kelton would say. *Ah!* brother." Stelton sighed deeply, which made Simon think of his own brothers kilometres and miles, even worlds away. He wondered if they were still alive, if they still survived the harsh conditions of the mines of Vendor.

"Tickthith, I want you to fly as far above us as you can. Make no sound. Keep watch. The Dark Prince may not be about, but he has many evil minions."

"Yes my lord," replied the guard.

Stelton and Simon continued to walk side by side, deeper and deeper into the darkness, descending further into the earth below. Simon looked at the prince out of the corner of his eye. He stood three or more times Simon's own height. His broad shoulders were made even more wide by the thick cloak of wings that fell down his back. Stelton kept one hand on the hilt of his sword whose red stones also glowed in the dark. Simon noticed that he walked mostly with his eyes closed, and opened them only when he spoke to Simon. When he closed his eyes his nose, which was small and fleshy and almost beak-like, scrunched up toward his eyes. Simon guessed that this was how he made his inaudable sounds.

Simon stopped walking and turned to look up into Stelton's face. "Stelton, before we go any further, I want to tell you that I'm very sorry about your brother. He saved my life. I didn't know him for very long, but he was very kind to me when I was in Melchura. He reminds me of my older brothers. They were never mean to me, like some kids' brothers were. I may never see them again either. I know how sad it can be."

Stelton bowed his head. "Thank you Simon. That means a lot to me. You know, I didn't think I would ever see Kelton again, but I did. So, do not give up hope. Always allow for the possiblity of hope, even if it feels like a far off dream. It grieves me to say such hope in me was gone when finally my brother and I did meet. I feared to meet him again, that he would be a Dryling different from the one I knew and loved. And yet my suspicions of him were entirely wrong. The tremendous anguish I felt all these years was energy wasted, the hope that has replaced it so good and whole. Yes, Simon, if you learn anything from me, learn from what now I understand as my painful mistake: never give up hope."

Stelton looked down at Simon and smiled, then he started to walk again. "Now, child, you must tell me something. How did you find my lost brothers?"

Simon raised his eyebrows and whistled. "Well, I hope to show you. But, it wasn't me who found them. I was brought to them, someone guided me."

"Who?" asked the Dryling prince.

"Follow me, and if it's not too late, I'll introduce you to him."

Chapter Twenty

It was morning again. Jill stayed at King Eckwith's side and watched as his condition worsenened all through the previous day and into the night. The wounds from the Dark Prince went deep, the members of the office of healers in the King's court were unable to treat them. At the king's request, Jill stayed at his side and told him stories about her life in Vendor, things about her world, and as much as she could remember about the Keeper's house in the Great Forest. When the guards appeared from behind the waterfall to report that the ruined gemstone left Simon, Tickthith and Stelton without any known passage back to Acchora, the King's spirits were crushed. He sat on his perch, chin curled into his chest, repeatedly moaning the names of his sons.

Jill looked upon the King with sadness, unable to offer any words of comfort. She simply sat beside him and held his hand.

"The names of your brave sons will be on the lips of our people for ages to come, great King, but now you must speak other words. You must name a successor to sit on your throne, for the days ahead are dark, and your people need a leader who can guide them."

Jill looked up and saw Olmander hovering outside the nest. How long she had sat there listening to the King's lament, she could not say. The thought that Olmander had sat and listened for some time watching her gave Jill the chills.

"With all sympathy, dear King, consider the fate of your people. What will happen if you leave a vacant throne?"

"Sympathy?" The female Dryling above Jill and the King dropped like a lightning bolt from the high branch where she had perched all through the night. She stood between the King and his newly arrived guest.

King Eckwith filled his chest with air and arched his shoulders. He no longer looked sick or weak. "And who would you suggest take the place of my son?"

Olmander raised his thick left eyebrow but said nothing.

"Oh come on, Olmander, you've been eyeing the throne for years. It's no secret. Do you really think you can lead the Drylings? You would shut us out to Acchora and to other worlds, hole us up in this prison until we are forgotten and erased from their memory forever. You will not lead the people, but bury them in the ground. We cannot stay in this mountain forever; we have remained in it for too long."

"Juria," said the King, "Olmander is a trusted member of the Council and has served the King for years. Show him the respect he deserves."

"'The respect he deserves?' I'm sorry, King Eckwith. I love you and our people too much to listen to such nonsense, this –"

"King Eckwith" Olmander interupted. "I did not come here to waste time playing games with her. I have never been known to waste words, you know that. You are dying. Your son Stelton may never return."

Juria spun and lunged toward Olmander. The King intervened. With surprising speed he stood and grabbed Juria by the arm. He held her tightly in his grip until she relaxed her body and calmed down. Juria looked angrily at Olmander, hands clenched into fists.

"How dare you speak to the King like that! How dare you –"

"Juria!" King Eckwith said and touched her gently on the shoulder. "Juria, it's okay. Olmander means no harm. He may not be very tactful, but his input is important. Please child, return to your post. You forget yourself, acting and speaking so reck-lessly. Please return to your post."

Juria reluctantly glided up to her post, high in the tree. The King sat back down on his perch. Olmander frowned. Jill watched the Dryling carefully.

"The throne must be filled," Olmander said. He looked up at Juria then back at the King. His voice dropped into an urgent whisper. "The Drylings need a clear successor to the throne. Who else in the kingdom has the memory of our race or the authority to lead?"

King Eckwith sighed and hunched over his perch. "I humbly offer my services to the Drylings in these terrible times."

Jill turned and watched the King. She could see no emotion in his face. The sadness and despair were gone, as was the quick readiness to smile.

"On behalf of the people, Olmander, I thank you for your generous offer of service."

With that, Olmander bowed his head and flapped his wings. In a matter of seconds, the old Dryling was at the entrance of the chamber. After a few moments of silence, the King slowly stood. Jill saw that he was in pain, but he ignored it.

"Juria, come here at once," he commanded, looking up to the branches. In an instant the Dryling was in the nest.

"I can't believe that old fool!" she began.

"Juria!"

"Who does he think he is?"

"Juria, I have heard enough from you. You must remember that Olmander is not the enemy, no Dryling is, not even those who long to see my line give up the throne. Not even those Drylings who helped the Rashtakar in his terrible war against us. They were tricked and deceived." The King pointed at the chamber. "The real enemy is this place. Inside

241

it we will always be his prisoners. Until we leave it, we will never be free."

King Eckwith leaned against the side of his nest and looked at the waterfall. Slowly, quietly, he began to laugh. Jill looked up at Juria who was also puzzled. The King finally turned to her and asked, "what would you have done to him if I had not stopped you?"

Juria blushed.

"Did you see his face?" King Eckwith asked.

"He looked scared," Jill said.

"Terrified," said the King, who continued to laugh. "Ah, Juria, I will always remember the look on his face." The King kissed her gently on the head. "Thank you."

Juria smiled and fought off a chuckle. "King Eckwith," asked the she-Dryling, "what will you do?"

"I think you know the answer already, it is what propelled you from your perch. It was for that love and loyalty that you spoke so bluntly to Olmander."

"Ama?" Juria asked, stepping toward the King and clasping his arms.

"Yes, my beloved Ama. The fate of our people has been accelerating to this moment with much speed. For weeks now the suspicion has been on my mind, and only now do I clearly understand the messengers the Guardian has been sending to me. We must summon her at once."

*　　*　　*

"Jill Strong, it is with utmost pride that I introduce you to my daughter, Ama, first of the Lightwings, princess of Acchora."

A veil divided the small chamber in which King Eckwith, Juria, and Jill stood. Ama slowly appeared from behind it, turned her head to the side and bowed. Jill was amazed at her beauty. She was tall like her father, but her features were softer, finer. Wings sloped gracefully off her shoulders; her fleshy beak-like nose was elongated and thin, and blue eyes the colour of sky filled the room with light. Ama's feathers were white and clean as freshly fallen snow. Her beauty seemed even more magical to Jill because she was not wholly visible. She appeared from behind the veil like an apparition, an angelic vision from another world.

"It's an honour to meet you," Jill said.

Ama smiled, touched Jill on the cheek, but did not say a word.

"I didn't know the King had a daughter," Jill said. "Have you been away, Ama?"

Ama smiled but remained silent. Jill looked at the King and then back at his daughter.

"Child, my daughter will not speak to you, she cannot speak. But soon that will change. It has been far too long since these halls heard the sweet voice of their most beautiful daughter."

"Is she still under the curse?" Jill asked, suddenly concerned.

"Oh no, it's nothing like that. She's under a vow, a vow she willingly took when she was a very young girl. Few in the kingdom remember my daughter, Jill, and you are one of the first to see her. Beyond members of the King's closest family, the only other individual to see her is Juria, who has been her attendant and servant all these years. Ama was the first female Dryling to be born in the kingly line, and belongs to the first generation that was born once we had been freed from the Rashtakar's curse. Her mother, my dear wife, died before Ama hatched."

Jill looked at Ama, then at the King. "I'm sorry," she said.

"We knew it would be that way," said the King. "You see, Ama's mother was very intuitive, more so than any other Dryling I have ever known. She was often visited by messegners of the Guardian. Before Ama emerged as a hatchling, her mother knew the kingdom awaited its first princess and that its first princess would not know her own mother. From the moment she hatched, Ama was set apart, one of a very few Drylings in our history who have taken strict vows. Her mother believed that the Guardian had special purposes for Ama, and that at the right time, her father would release her from her vow to share it with Acchora." A single tear clouded King Eckwith's eye and traced a mark down his feathered cheek. "Today, daughter, the time has come. Tonight I will free you from your vow, and tonight you will share what wisdom you have received from all your years of solitude and silence."

Chapter Twenty-One

Simon stopped walking and sat down with Stelton on a large rock to rest. Somewhere, out of sight, Tickthith hovered nearby. The cavern was cold; currents of air rushed through unseen crevices of rock making hollow whispering sounds, as though a large mouth sucked cold air into giant lungs. Simon had walked in silence for hours with Stelton, stopping only for a few hours to rest and sleep. The red glow of light illuminated a sphere of space a few feet around him on all sides. Stelton made Simon stop every once in awhile to rest and snack on the crunchy round seeds and sip on the water he brought with him and carried under his cloak, along with a reserve of dried fish that Simon continued to refuse and would refuse until "it was absolutely necessary."

"Tell me, young Simon, how you came to our world and how you found the Drylings that are under the ground. Fill this eerie silence with a story."

"I was never good at telling stories," Simon said to the prince.

"That's alright," said Stelton. "Just do your best to tell me what happened."

"Well, to be honest, Stelton, Jill and I never meant to come here at all. It was sort of an accident. Has Jill already told you about the wheel and the water and our search on the beach?"

Stelton nodded his head.

"Jill was given a treasure to keep by someone very important where we come from, ten silver coins that she wasn't supposed to let anyone touch or see. She dropped her bag of coins onto the ground when we were in the Great Hall, and somehow, one slipped into your world. I don't know how we got here, it was some kind of magic, and ever since I've been here, things have happened that I can't explain. All because of one silly little coin. I don't know how, but I think the coin somehow changed when we entered Acchora. The creature that led me down here, the one that pulled me into the ground, he found the treasure and put it on his finger as a ring. That is part of the story I can't tell you about. All I know is that we thought we had found the treasure, and the next thing we knew, we had found a ring attached to a hand, a hand that pulled me underneath the ground.

"That creature brought me here, he led me through darkness far below the earth. He held onto my hand once we passed through the sand and would not let go. It was so dark, I could not see. He wouldn't tell me his name, the only words he said he repeated over and over again. He repeated them so often, he nearly drove me crazy: *Down, down, down. Further, deeper. Below rock, and time, and sound. For this I was made, to find my place, be buried in the ground and die.* At first the words sent chills down my spine, but he repeated them so often, they lost their creepiness. He was such a strange creature, his skin so white I could see him in the dark; it was like seeing a fish in a pool of water at night, kind of like following the shadow of a ghost. I was terrified of him at first. When I realized he wasn't going to hurt me, I was no longer afraid, just confused where he was taking me, and sad that he wanted to die.

"We walked through darkness for many, many hours, maybe days. I don't know. Too long to count. Only darkness and that faint silver-white shadow. No sleep. At times I wondered if I was still alive or if I had, in fact died myself, and now passed through some terrible afterlife. There are stories of similar fates where I come from, I always hated them. But then, suddenly I could see more light, torches lined the walls and we found ourselves in a chamber. It was there I met Kelton, your brother. I had never seen such an amazing creature before, a sort of frightening and powerful angel. An enormous talking bird-creature that I would compare to an eagle in my world. The first thing he did was extend his hand and welcome me. He said, 'You have arrived.' He expected us. The Guardian, he said, had told him we would come."

"My brother spoke with the Guardian?"

"Voices. His messengers. He explained it to me, but I never really understood what he was talking about."

"My brother heard from the Guardian? I can hardly believe it. He was always such a skeptic when he lived in Acchora, he made fun of me for wanting to listen for the messengers."

"I understand why, it all sounded a little strange to me."

"And you say you could always see him? His body wasn't invisible or transparent like mine?"

"No, I was always able to see him and the other Drylings."

"Fascinating. Your arrival in our world, Simon, was no accident. What did he tell you about the Guardian? Once you arrived, what did you do?"

"We waited. The creature sat in the chamber against a wall and didn't move. I sat with your brother and his wife and children."

"Children!" Stelton said looking beyond Simon, into the darkness. After a few moments of quietness, Stelton asked, "what, exactly, were you waiting for?"

"We didn't know. Your brother only knew what the messengers had told him: they would have two visitors, then the Rashtakar would come and cause the Drylings to suffer some more. Then, they would go home."

*   *   *

"Drylings of Acchora, I present to you my daughter Ama Lightwing, long exiled in solitude, hidden from her people, ever to be loved by you and known as princess."

Astonishment rushed over the crowd who had gathered in the great stalactite chamber awaiting an announcement from the King. It was rare in Acchora for the King to address at one time all those hidden under the mountain. Rumours began to travel quickly through the underground vents and holes, the most common one being that the King would announce a successor, and though he was not a popular figure with most Drylings in Acchora, many expected Olmander would be named King in Stelton's absence.

King Eckwith waited for the initial shock of his announcement to wane. He smiled to himself, aware that Ama was a sudden and surprising revelation. Four of the King's guard entered the chamber from a high vent in the ceiling, from the stalactites above. Each Dryling faced a different direction: north, south, east, and west. And in their hands, which were raised above their heads, they each held the corners of a long purple cloth. The Drylings fell from the vent and pulled the cloth with them, forming a four sided chamber that fell from the ceiling.

Jill stood beside the King on a raised platform and watched as the cloth dropped from the roof. The King unsheathed his sword and held it in the air. On this cue, the four descending Drylings separated in four different directions to the edges of the chamber.

When they did, white flowers, petals spinning in soft arcs, fell from the chamber ceiling and floated to the ground. Jill gasped at the sight, and when Ama appeared among the flowers, wings spread above her shoulders as she descended from the high vent to her father, all the Drylings went onto one knee.

King Eckwith leaned toward his daughter and kissed her on the cheek. He then touched the hilt of his sword to her lips and placed the blade in her outstretched hands. In one voice, the crowd shouted, "Hail Ama, Queen of Achorra! Hail Ama, Queen!"

When Ama was seated with her father, King Eckwith looked at Jill and winked. Jill went to the edge of the platform and addressed the crowd, words she had rehearsed over and over again in the last few hours.

"Drylings of Acchora. The King greets you and wishes you prosperity. It is my great honour to speak for the King who has taken his own vow of silence, a symbolic gesture to show the voice of the Drylings is now the voice of his daughter, Queen Ama. May her reign surpass the greatness of her ancestors and may you obey her as Queen, even unto death. Drylings of Acchora, what do you say?"

The Drylings stood, hands over their hearts, and said, "So be it! Ama is our Queen!"

Jill took a deep breath, thankful that the Drylings had responded as they did. King Eckwith assured her they would know what to do, but Jill feared silence and blank, nervous faces.

"And now, Drylings of Acchora," Jill continued. "Your majesty, the Queen."

The Drylings were quiet, the air electric with anticipation, every one aware that the new Queen was speaking for the first in a very long time. Ama stood from her seat and slowly walked over to Jill. Jill bowed her head then slowly stepped to King Eckwith's side. Ama raised her chin, looked over the crowd, then closed her eyes. For a number of moments she said nothing. When she looked over the crowd she spoke in a clear, steady voice.

"My beloved people. It is with great joy and some sadness that I speak to you today. For a long time I have awaited this moment, to meet you, to see you. Many times I have longed to end my vow of silence and live among you. Today is bittersweet, for it is a day that marks the end of my father's illustrious reign. Bittersweet because my heart warms to see you, yet it is the last time I will speak to you, at least for a long while. I have only now met you, and now I must leave. For, my time to visit the land of the Guardian has finally come. The story of our race has been dark and difficult and for this reason many doubt Acchora and the Drylings have been watched by the Guardian at all. To such skeptics I can only say I strongly and forever disagree.

"During my years of silence I have been sure of one thing. The Guardian is real, and he calls me to himself. For what purpose I am not certain, and for how long I do not know. But I do know this: I must go to him, and I do so for my people. Though you and I may not understand why, it must be done. My

vow must be fulfilled. I will join Jill Strong on a
journey to Terador, for in the last days of my silence
it became clear to me that we are to share the road
together.

"I consider it my duty to lead you as my father
before me, but my duty to the Guardian must
surpass all things. My father's days are short, there-
fore, I must also soon announce a successor to the
throne who will lead you in the tradition of my
ancestors: with justice and kindness. Tomorrow Jill
Strong will act as my mouthpiece and announce to
you my decision.

"For one glorious moment I sat on the throne
of my father. It was a dream that faded too quickly.
Dear Drylings, I see the sadness on your faces and
wish I could change it. My heart breaks. One day
those hearts will be filled with hope again, and on
that day I will live among you at last. I long for that
day, but still, it must wait. Drylings farewell."

Ama turned, walked to her father, and kissed
him on the cheek. King Eckwith did not move. He
sat on his perch, stunned. Juria came to Ama's side
and escorted her to the side of the platform and
through the passageway into the inner chamber of
the King, now her private dwelling. Jill touched the
King's hand; it was cold and trembled. She looked
out at the crowd and saw the same thing: Drylings
stuck in place, amazed at what they heard, thinking
deeply about what Ama just said, replaying her
words in their minds.

Olmander flew toward the platform and stopped
short of it. Members of the King's guard quickly

withdrew their swords and stood in front of the King. Olmander hovered in the air and put up his hands.

"A word with the King," he said.

"King Eckwith is under a vow of silence," replied one of the guards "His vow is binding and will not be broken. He can speak to no Dryling."

Olmander squinted his eyes and looked at Jill. "Can he speak with her?"

"If he chooses," replied the guard.

Olmander shook his head and cursed under his breath. Two guards helped King Eckwith to his feet, and pulled Jill in their tow. They slowly made their way toward the Royal chamber.

"What are you up to, you little witch?" he yelled at Jill as they walked away. "What are you scheming? King, she cannot be trusted. Guards!" Olmander started for his sword which was sheated under his wing. A guard struck him on the mouth and pinned him against the ground.

"The girl is a trusted friend and ally. The King will have no evil words spoken of her, especially from you Olmander. Be at peace."

Jill matched the pace of the guards who carried King Eckwith, frightened and angry by Olmander's outburst. When she crossed into the darkness of the passage to the Royal chamber, Jill stole a look behind her. A small crowd of Drylings had gathered around Olmander and were helping him to his feet. The old creature looked in Jill's direction and spit onto the ground.

Chapter Twenty-Two

T he downward path Simon walked on started to level out and even as his eyes were making out the faint trace of light in the distance he heard Tickthith's voice which pulled him from his dream of cold and darkness.

"Master, ahead of us, the path opens into a chamber. I think we have come to it at last!"

"How can it be?" asked Stelton. "I sense no one at all. Tickthith?"

"Me either, Master. Nothing."

"Simon," said Stelton, "draw your sword and cover the light. I want you to wait here in the dark, by these rocks. We will go in and survey the chamber so we can plan what offensive we can risk against our enemy."

"Okay," Simon said, unable to mask his disappointment.

"Simon, is there anything you can tell us about Melchura?"

"There are a number of chambers and passage-ways. The main chamber which lays ahead of us is where the Dark Prince stays when he visits. In the back of it is a cave with a lot of gemstones and mirrors. He showed it to me before we went to Achorra, he said each mirror represented one of his worlds. There are two larger chambers on either side of the cave. One chamber led to the mineral beds where Drylings were sent to work. The other is the chamber where your people were forced to live. That's where I arrived first."

"Tickthith, let's go. We will fly among the stalactites where we will be difficult to see. Simon, we will call for you when it is safe."

"Be careful," Simon whispered as Stelton pushed off the ground and joined Tickthith in the air.

Simon sat in the darkness, his back against a rock. He strained to listen for the sound of clashing swords. He heard nothing. His legs and arms were numb with cold where he sat motionless. As he massaged his aching limbs, he remembered his fear when he saw the first hideous creatures that worked for the Dark Prince, the ones that found him among the Drylings soon after his arrival. Their terrible faces, carnivorous and wolf-like, were gnarled in a permanent expression of cruelty. When they noticed him, they ran to him and surrounded him in a pack, growling and whispering in different languages. Occasionally he could hear them throw insults at him in English; they said very cruel things, and threatened to harm him. The whole time he remained in Melchura, however, they did not touch him. They were like bullies at the playground at school: cruel and mean but afraid to do any real harm. The creatures were too afraid of the Dark Prince to act out their violent impulses against Simon, lest their Master do greater violence against them. But if they were permitted, Simon knew the creatures would not hesitate to tear him limb from limb.

The creatures were terrifying to look at, but their smell was the worst: garbage, and feces, and rotten meat. Smells that assaulted Simon and made him feel nauseous and sick. The insults and threats were awful at first, but soon he learned to ignore them, especially when he realized they could do nothing but what the Dark Prince permitted. The smell, *oh the smell!* it never went away.

Simon stood to his feet with a start and moved toward the chamber. Stelton had not called, but he knew they were in no danger from the Dark Prince and his foul servants: there was no trace of their horrible smell the whole journey from Achorra to Melchura, and no scent of them where he waited in the dark, so near to the chamber where they would be. The Dark Prince and his servants were gone!

Simon heard cries from within the chamber that echoed off the cavern walls and up along the path he and Stelton had descended. Simon started to run and, dagger in hand, was quickly in the main chamber. The faint light he had seen from outside came from various torches that still burned along the walls. Most were extinguished or had recently burnt out. Traces of smoke from the torches filled the room. Another cry sounded, deep and full of anguish.

"Stelton? Tickthith?" Simon's voice echoed throughout the empty chamber. No living thing was within sight.

"No! It can't be! No, Tickthith!" Simon heard the cry and turned about in the room, following the echoing cry as it reverberated off rock and moved out of the chamber. Simon felt dizzy at the sound, which seemed to echo and resonate in his head, fill his body with anxiety, and disorient him where he stood. "No! No!" Stelton continued to scream, and the echoes continued to mash and tangle through Simon's senses. Simon covered his ears with his hands and started to move toward the cave at the end of the chamber.

Simon passed a few of the mirrors and gemstones that the Dark Prince had so proudly shown to Simon. They were smashed. Pieces of coloured rock and glass were strewn along the cave floor. Few hung in their place. Someone had destroyed them. Simon spun on his heel and ran into the Dryling's living chamber. When he passed into it, he discovered the source of the screams, and his heart stopped. Dryling bodies covered the ground, it was impossible to even see the floor of the chamber. Everywhere he looked fallen Drylings lay lifeless, as though everyone in the room had decided to go to sleep. Thick orange-yellow blood covered their bodies and collected at their throats and chests where they had been pierced by swords. The room was quiet and impossibly still but for Stelton who held a Dryling in his arms and screamed in anguish. Tickthith merely stood, motionless and dumb.

Simon could hardly breathe, he dropped his sword on the ground and stepped backward, his feet tripping over a dead Dryling. He lost his balance and fell onto a young Dryling whose eyes stared blankly up at the ceiling, its body stiff, hands frozen around its throat nearly covering the terrible wound. Simon fumbled and scrambled on the ground, falling over bodies, trying to stand up, afraid to touch them, unable to find his feet.

"Oh no, help, I'm sorry!" Simon breathed, crawling over bodies looking for any sign of life. "There must be some! No one could be so evil, no one would kill all of them, not even him, not even him." Simon started to shout. "Hello? Can you hear me? Where are you, we can help! Sit up and we'll help you! Please! Someone."

Simon came to a place on the ground where there was only rock. He sat down, pulled his knees into his chest and closed his eyes. He tried to control his breathing but could not. He tried to sit still but his body shook all over. His face was hot and all strength left his body. Simon heard a voice, and looked over toward Stelton. The Prince was no longer yelling, but held out his hand to Simon with a look of the most exquisite and painful sadness on his face.

Simon slowly stood and carefully stepped toward the Dryling prince. Stelton pulled Simon into his body and covered the boy with his wings so that he could no longer see the death all around him.

"Child –"

"Stelton, they're all dead. All of them. All your friends."

"I know, Simon. I know. I can't believe it. How could he have done this? His capacity for evil is greater than any of us imagined."

"Stelton," said Simon, "I'm afraid. Afraid I'll go insane. The death in this room is too much, it's going to kill me."

"I know, Simon. I'm so sorry. No one, whether young or old should ever see such horror. This evil is unspeakable, there is no reaction to it but despair. I don't know what to do, but here, stay with me, underneath my wings. We won't move until we can think, okay? You're safe with me."

*   *   *

How long he stayed in that protective shelter, Simon would never know, for time was suspended by the cruel confusion of grief. Whenever he closed his eyes, Simon could again see the vacant desperation in the eyes of the dead and could only imagine the horrors they expereinced even as they breathed their last breaths. And just when the despair of such thoughts began to overwhelm him like a flood, Simon would open his eyes and look into Stelton's. And it was those eyes that sustained him, though they too were weighed with grief. Like lights that burned as candles in darkness, honest in their despair yet marked by a glimmer of something rich and deep, Stelton's eyes comforted Simon and promised him it was possible to be saved from the finality of such darkness.

When Simon finally nodded his head at Stelton whose patience could have lasted a hundred years, the Dryling put a hand on the boy's shoulder then unfurled his wings. The chamber had changed. The floor was cleared of bodies, but for the furtherst wall where Tickthith had lined them in four long rows. Stelton looked at Simon and told him he could come over to the bodies or stay where he stood, or leave the chamber and wait outside.

Simon stayed with Stelton as he walked between rows of bodies and told Simon their names, Drylings he had not seen in years, brothers and sisters he once thought dead. But there were many more Drylings that he had never seen, and for these Drylings, born in captivity, he kneeled beside them and sang a prayer. One of these songs was interrupted by a familiar voice.

"Master Stelton, come at once, look what I have found!"

Stelton looked up and saw Tickthith standing at the chamber door. His body, face, and feathers were covered in dirt and blood from the removal of bodies. In his hand he held a round white object.

"Where did you find that?" Stelton asked, grabbing Simon and flying over to the chamber entrance.

"In the other chamber, in the cleft of a rock. There are more."

"How many?" Stelton asked, clutching Tickthith's forearms.

"Three that were whole. There were many, but most were broken or crushed. I found three altogether that are whole. And there's something else you might want to see."

"Is that what I think it is?" asked Simon.

"Yes," Stelton said, a smile breaking through the darkness of grief overwhelming the cavern like a beam of sunlight through grey cloud. "Eggs! Take us to them at once!"

*   *   *

The path through to the other chamber was somewhat treacherous. Simon walked slowly, holding the red rock light Stelton had given him earlier. The rocks they walked on were very wet and slippery, the pathway led deeply into the ore mines where the Dark Prince forced the Drylings to work. Finally, Tickthith picked Simon up off the ground and flew him with great speed to a place far inside the chamber, Stelton followed closely behind.

"Here, at the end of this passageway," Tickthith said.

They flew a little further, then stopped and touched onto the ground. Egg shells lined the ground among the rocks, it looked as though they had been thrown and stomped on.

"Who would do such a thing, kill innocent hatchlings?" Stelton said under his breath. "Tickthith, where are the others?"

"At the end of the path. He wouldn't let me take them."

"Who wouldn't let you?" Stelton asked.

"The creature."

"One of the Rashtakar's?" Stelton asked, putting his hand to his sword.

"I don't think so" said Tickthith.

"It's him, isn't it?" asked Simon. "It's the creature that brought me here."

The trio walked a little further and came to the end of the path.

"Watch out young Simon," said Tickthith. "Careful that you don't fall. The path drops into a shaft. He's up there on the ledge. Raise your light and you will see."

Simon raised the red light into the air. The shadow of his head and arm stretched and projected onto the cavern wall in front of him where he could see a faint white form, like the slick under-belly of a fish glimmering in a dark pool of water. Simon called out to the creature then listened for a response. It took him a few moments to hear the sound of slow, laboured breathing beyond the rapid beating of his own heart.

"What is its name?" Stelton asked.

"I don't know," Simon shrugged his shoulders, whispering. "He spoke very little, and when he did speak it was always the same thing. I don't think he has a name." Simon stepped closer to the crevasse and raised his light. "Come on now, creature, don't you recognize my voice? It's Simon, your friend who walked with you all the way down to this awful world."

"It looks like he's hurt," Stelton said, pointing at the creature.

"He is, Master," Tickthith replied. "I found this one egg here on the shelf beside him. I think he left it because it is no longer a living hatchling. The shell has softened and is cold. The other two, I think he is holding onto, to ensure they survive. He must have escaped with them from the chamber of death then came here to save these young lives. I don't think he's dangerous, but he might think that we are."

"Take me up to him, Stelton," Simon said.

Stelton picked Simon up and flew up to the ledge. The creature cowered in the corner against the rockface. He held two rather large eggs to his chest and put them between him and the wall.

"Dear creature, did you protect these young hatchlings from the hand of the Rashtakar and his beasts?" Stelton asked.

The creature nodded.

"These eggs belong to me. I am Stelton Greywing, Prince of Acchora, I come to take my lost brothers home."

Stelton held out his hand. The creature slowly turned from the wall and faced Stelton. The creature's body was oddly shaped and very white, it reminded Simon very much of a beluga whale, though he was much smaller and had two arms and two legs. The creature was not much larger than Simon was tall, but he was twice as wide as the

boy. His stocky legs looked almost reptilian, thick
with muscle where they attached to his torso, they
kept him low to the ground, bent and balanced over
long thighs and shins connected by bony knees. To
Simon, he looked like a blob of white flesh hunched
over muscled legs. He could hardly make out any
shape of abdomen, shoulders, or neck. His head,
only distinguishable because of dark round eyes,
pointed toward the ground. A small mouth with
sharp little teeth twisted sideways into a kidney-
shaped hole was offset on the right side of his face.
Thin arms with four spidery fingers portruded from
his side, and under these were the Dryling eggs.
Simon could make little sense of the body, in no
way did it seem symmetrical to him, but like an
unfinished beluga fetus whose body looked more
like a tumor than anything else. Even in the dim
light, Simon could see the ring on the second finger
of the creature's right hand glimmer in the red light.

Slowly, the creature shuffled over to Stelton
and handed him the eggs. Stelton put Simon on the
ledge and took the eggs. He cradled them to his
chest, leaned over and kissed each egg gently.

"You've kept them very warm. You saved both
their lives. On behalf of my people I thank you."

"Creature, you're hurt!" Simon said as he
noticed the thick gash across it's lower body. "How
long have you been down here?" Simon asked and
touched the wound. It left a thick marshmallow goo
on his hand. "Stelton, we need to get him out of
here, or he'll die."

At the word, the creature's eyes flashed in the red light. He looked at Simon with what could only be described as a smile.

"Die," it gasped, a throaty sound as air sucked through the twisted hole of a mouth.

"We'll do everything we can to save you," Stelton said. "Tickthith, carry him. We must take him out of the chamber. It's too cold in here, he won't last long."

The creature grabbed Simon by the shoulders and pulled him into his chest. He grabbed Simon's hand and thrust it against his wound.

"Down, down, down!" it shouted. "Further, deeper."

"His wound, Stelton! He's trying to open it. Can you pull him away from me? He'll make his injuries worse!"

Tickthith came to Simon's aide and tried to pull the creature's grip loose.

"Below rock, and time, and sound," it moaned.

"It's no use, Master. He's too strong. Simon, are you okay? It looks like he's crushing you."

"It doesn't hurt that badly. Creature, why are you doing this to yourself?"

"Further, deeper," it repeated, it's voice softer now. "Down, down, down. For this I was made, to find my place, be buried in the ground and die."

"Creature!" Simon shouted, as his hand was pulled further into the gooy softness. Simon tried to pull his arm out of the creature's side, but he had too little strength.

"Deeper down, down," it gasped, "ground, ground, gr –" and then it spoke no more.

Suddenly Simon felt the full weight of the creature against his body and staggered along the ledge. His legs started to cramp beneath him, then gave out altogether. He hit the rock and rolled over the edge. Cold air rushed against his back and, suddenly, he was weightless, falling into the black void of the crevasse. Before he could call for help, he felt strong arms under him.

"I have you!" Tickthith shouted and snatched Simon out of the air. He pulled the creature off of the boy and carried them under separate arms. "No more death today, Simon. It stops here."

Tickthith carried Simon and the creature back through the passageway to the mouth of the cave where the Dark Prince had his lair. Stelton followed behind, and when they were at the threshold of the chamber that held the bodies of their fallen kinsman, Tickthith put Simon back onto the ground.

"He's dead, then, isn't he?" Simon asked to no one in particular.

"It looks like he finally got his wish," Stelton said, shaking his head.

"What a shame," replied Simon. He looked up at Stelton. "What do we do now?"

"I think we must honour his wish; we must bury him in the ground."

"Right here?" Simon asked.

"I think he wanted it that way. We don't bury our dead, we burn them. We have a lot of funerals to conduct today. We cannot leave this place until we have properly honoured the dead."

"Then what? Where will we go?" asked Simon. "How do we get out of here?"

Stelton looked up at the cavern celing, then at the walls.

"I don't know Simon. I don't know."

Chapter Twenty-Three

"**B**ut you heard what he called me! How can I go out there and stand before your people and tell them who you have chosen as their new Queen?"

"Jill, it is the way it must be. You are here for a reason. My family needs you. My father needs you. Just like your mother before you, you have come to help our people."

Jill bit her tongue. She was not angry at Ama or King Eckwith, she was just angry. *Olmander thinks I'm a worse witch than she!* was what she wanted to shout at the Queen, the very statement she imagined the whole kingdom of Acchora now believed, if Olmander had his way.

"And what if they don't accept your decision?" Jill asked, when she had regained some of her composure.

"They will not accept it, that I already know," Queen Ama replied.

Jill was dumbfounded. She stepped to the edge of the Royal Perch and dangled her arms over the side. She looked down to the bottom of the tree. Jill, Ama, and the King all stood in the nest, and it seemed much smaller as a result. Juria was stationed high in a branch in the tree, and members of the Royal guard were positioned at the chamber's entrance, swords in hand.

"Will there be a war?" Jill asked.

"We hope it won't come to that, but it might." King Eckwith said, sadly. "If it comes to that, my dear child, then you know what you must do."

"I don't understand, King Eckwith. You're willing to destroy your people's way of life? Isn't that the very thing that the Rashtakar wanted to do all along? What will you accomplish by driving your people from this place?"

"Then they will finally be free. We must leave this place, we've already talked about it, Jill."

"But why me? If you're so certain, why don't you drop the stone?" Jill said, folding her arms across her chest and facing the King.

"Because," Ama said, standing beside Jill and touching her cheek, "the Guardian would have it that way. We love our world enough to ruin it so that it can be changed. But he has given you the authority to shatter it."

"This sounds like a very bad dream," Jill said, rubbing her temples. "How can you be so sure about this?" she asked.

"Because we have heard from the Guardian, we have listened to his messages," Ama replied.

"But what if you heard wrong?" Jill asked.

"That's a possibility."

"It's a possiblity and you're still going to go ahead and ruin your world? That's crazy? Don't you think you should be sure?"

"Hearing from the Guardian always presents that sort of risk, for we are imperfect creatures still learning to hear."

"What if you heard wrong!"

"I have not," Ama said. She smiled, then hugged her arms to her chest.

"Jill, this is very hard to understand," said King Eckwith. "We see our people who, under the leadership of Olmander, would choose to live in the comfort of these caves rather than live in the light of day where they were meant to live, only to avoid an inevitable war with their real enemy. We do not want to see Drylings go to war with each other, especially over a place that was never really meant to be their home. Even if we did not hear properly from the Guardian, though we believe we heard correctly, we still think it best to force the people's hand, drive them from this place, and make them face their real enemy. The Rashtakar has evil creatures that rule the land and sea of Achorra, and they have ruled it for too long. Your mother, Jill –"

"Many Drylings think my mother was a witch –"

"That, dear child, is a lie!" The King shouted. He took a breath, pressed his hands against his legs then continued. "It is a lie you must never believe. Your mother spoke of a time when we would have our voice and our bodies again. Her words are in line with the messages Ama and I have been receiving from the Guardian and his messages coincide with your arrival in our world. The time is right, Jill. The fruit is ripe."

"My arrival here was an accident. I came here because I wasn't careful. I came here –" Jill stopped and shook her head. She was so frustrated she could cry, but too angry to break down in front of the King and his daughter. "Ah! I don't know why I came here anymore."

"You came here because you heard a voice like the one that we have heard," Ama said. "You responded to that voice. Now we do the same."

Jill covered her face with her hands.

"It's all so infuriating," she said. "What if my actions cause Drylings to die? What if you're wrong?"

"What if we're right?" King Eckwith asked, then smiled. "Trust us, Jill. Trust us, or trust Olmander."

Jill looked at the King in surprise. The King raised his eyebrow and pursed his lips. Jill buried her face in her hands again and groaned.

"Enough said," was her reply.

"Good," said the King. "Here, then. Take this." King Eckwith handed Jill the red stone that had been buried under his nest. "You will know when to use it."

*   *   *

Ama, Jill, and Juria stood on the platform in the main chamber of the Dryling habitation and looked over the gathered crowd. Hundreds of Drylings gathered and quietly waited the announcement their new Queen promised to make. In front of the platform, on the ground, members of the Queen's guard were positioned, a normal sight at a coronation, but what the crowd did not know was that the guards were given orders to be ready to whisk the Queen and her companions away at a moment's notice. King Eckwith was not present, his health took a sharp turn for the worse just hours before the announcement was to be made. He lay in his nest, attended by healers in the Royal chamber, barely clinging to life.

Jill scanned the crowd. She was somewhat nervous, but when she decided to trust Ama and the King's judgment, she was visited with a very welcome sense of calm. Even Olmander could not unsettle it outright from where he sat near the front of the platform sneering at her. Ama looked at her, nodded, and Jill stepped to the front of the platform. As she did, she could not help thinking it strange that this was the second time in as many days that she had addressed an entire nation on behalf of royalty. Though she felt almost at home with the Drylings, the thought made her feel very far from home.

She began to say the words she had memorized. "Drylings of Acchora. The Queen greets you and wishes you prosperity. It is my great honour to speak as the mouthpiece for Queen Ama Lightwing, a task I was appointed for and carry out with great humility. This is a unique day for the Drylings. Your Prince and heir to the throne, Stelton of the Grey Wing is gone from us, and we do not know when or how he will return. Your Queen must also leave to lands beyond this one, for she is called by the Guardian himself; while she is gone, another must sit on her throne to rule the Drylings in justice and in peace. Queen Ama's one request is that you honour your new monarch with the love and respect you showed both her and her father."

Jill looked over the crowd who seemed to lean toward her, hanging on every word. She glanced at Olmander from the corner of her eye, then down at her feet. She took a deep breath.

"Now, it is with great pride that I present to you your new Queen, Juria of the Royal Guard, trusted friend and loyal servant of the Queen and her family. May her reign surpass the greatness of her ancestors and may you obey her as Queen, even unto death. Drylings of Acchora, what do you say?"

Jill looked over a silent crowd. Not a single Dryling moved or made a sound.

"Drylings of Acchora, what do you say?" she tried again.

Some of the Drylings dropped their heads, unable to look at Jill. Some looked up at Juria and the Queen. Many stared fixedly ahead, as if in a trance. Jill stole a look at Ama, who smiled at Jill and signaled for the girl to return to her side. Ama then took her sword, touched it to Juria's lips then placed the blade in her hand. She nodded to Juria

273

who stepped toward the front of the platform and looked at the people.

"Drylings of Acchora," she began, "I humbly accept the decision of Queen Ama to serve you as leader of this great race."

As she spoke, Olmander stood up and jumped into the air, unfurling his wings. "You are no Queen!" he shouted, "but a mere pawn in a foolish game that would keep Drylings with real authority from the power that is theirs to rule." Olmander then turned his back to Juria and faced the crowd. "Drylings of Acchora, these false monarchs on the platform only posture as royalty. Do not be deceived. Our King lies ill and against his wishes they try to supplant his kingdom. Wait and see! One of the first decisions that Juria will make is to force us to leave our homes and move above ground where we will be vulnerable to our enemy. And this wicked daughter of Eckwith plans to abandon us, knowing full well she flees to safer worlds, while she betrays her people and leaves them to die."

"Nonesense!" some shouted from the crowd.

"Hear, hear!" shouted others.

"Olmander, you are out of line," shouted Juria, above the crowd, who suddenly became silent.

"Clearly, Juria, I am. You have pushed me right out of line to the throne. You know I am the likeliest candidate. For I have served Ama's father as coun-selor throughout his reign. Why, Ama?" Olmander asked, pointing at her, "Why do you push me from the throne, tell your people."

"Would you force your Queen to break her vow of silence?" Jill asked.

"Who are you to interfere in the matters of the Drylings?" Olmander yelled back at Jill. "Answer me, Ama, Why do you push me from the throne? You owe it to your people to tell us. Do not hide behind your vow of silence!"

"I do not push you, Olmander," Ama said, breaking her silence. The crowd gasped. "I do not push you from the throne, but I do not choose you. You would love power more than you love the people. I do not choose you as King because I do not trust you to rule them."

Olmander laughed. "You see, Drylings? She is mad! She maligns me, and she maligns you and your homeland. She and her successor wish us to leave this safe mountain."

"But don't you see that we must?" Juria asked. "We must return to our proper place in the land of Acchora. We were not made to grovel and hide under rock like worms. We were meant to rule the land. We must take it from the Rashtakar once for all!"

"You see? See what they conspire? Will *she* lead us to war and victory, a victory we could not accomplish even under the leadership of Eckwith and his sons? Will a she-Dryling really lead us in war?"

Drylings throughout the crowd laughed at the thought, but others watched Juria closely, as if trying to decide if she meant what she said. The crowd was clearly split in opinion about who should rule.

Even as the crowd became more and more unsettled, a messenger from the Royal chamber flew onto the platform and whispered in a guard's ear. The guard dropped his head, slowly turned, and walked to Queen Ama. When he spoke with the Queen, she dropped her head. Ama stepped to the front of the platform and raised her arms in the air. The crowd quickly quieted.

"My beloved Drylings. It is with great sadness that I now address you. King Eckwith is dead."

The crowd gasped. Some Drylings fell to their faces on the ground and began to wail.

"No one mourns his passing more than I do," Ama continued, "but I must insist, that today we, together, recognize our new Queen, especially in light of this sad news. Let us honour my father with our choice. I shared my decision with him, and he blessed it. Drylings, obey the wishes of your Queen and her father. Do not add to the sadness of this day."

"How dare you!" shouted Olmander. "Do you see what she is doing, my people? Rather than mourn the death of her father, she turns his death into a political campaign. Drylings, it is I who should be King!" shouted Olmander. "I will lead you and you will be safe. I will not needlessly sacrifice your lives. And, I will properly honour the dead!"

Suddenly the crowd moved and shouted and was on its feet. Olmander drew his sword and faced the platform. Juria also pulled her sword, though Ama shouted in the noise for her to sheath it again.

The guards surrounding the platform leaped into the air, swords and shields in hand. Six guards, three on each side surrounded Juria, Ama, and Jill and quickly escorted them to the Royal chamber. A group of Drylings flew at the guards but were thrown back. Various groups throughout the crowd exchanged words, fists, and some swords.

"So it begins," Ama said, as she entered the Royal chamber. "So it begins."

*   *   *

Stelton and Tickthith returned to the main chamber. They went in with two burning torches, and came out with nothing in their hands. When they returned, they sealed the chamber's stone door shut.

"May they rest in peace," Simon said, smiling sadly.

"May they rest in peace," repeated the Drylings.

"While you were in the chamber, I decided to do my part. I found some soft ground and dug a hole. Can you help me put the creature's body in it?"

"We can," said Stelton.

"It doesn't seem right, though, to bury someone without a name," Simon said.

"Then why don't we name him?"

"Can we do that?" Simon asked.

"We can," replied Stelton.

"I don't know what type of creature he was, or where he even came from, but I think I want to name him Stanley Stewart, after my brothers, and

Kelton after yours, because I think he was both kind and brave."

"That sounds good to me," said Stelton.

Tickthith gently picked up the creature and placed him in the ground where Simon dug a hole. Stelton took the Dryling egg that did not survive in the cavern and kissed it, he then placed it beside the creature in the grave. "Thank you, creature, for saving two lives. Our people are united with you in death."

"Stanely Kelton Stewart," Simon said, "may you rest in peace."

Stelton put the other two eggs on the ground and bent down with Simon and Tickthith and began to cover the creature's body with earth.

*   *   *

Queen Ama!" shouted a guard over the noise in the Royal chamber, you must leave your father's side at once and command your troops. War is at our hands and we need you."

Queen Ama bent over her dead father and kissed him on the forehead. She looked at Jill who stood with her in her father's nest and smiled.

"Stay here, Jill, but be ready. The time to leave this place will come much sooner than even I expected."

With that, Ama dropped from sight and glided to the ground. Juria stood with sword in hand, her wings folded tightly against her back. She waited for Ama behind the line of guards standing at the entrance of the Royal chamber. Outside a clamour of noise could be heard. Olmander and a band of Drylings who considered him a better choice for ruler of Acchora attempted to break through the chamber door.

"Guards of the Royal family!" Ama shouted over the noise. "For a long time you have loyally served and protected my family. At this critical hour I ask not for the protection of myself, but of your people. You must fight for Acchora, and fight for her rightful Queen. For, long have you also served with Juria, a loyal servant of the kingdom. It is her I choose as Queen, and her you will serve. If you will not obey her, then give up your swords and walk behind that door. But know this, our stories will tell of your cowardice and betrayal, and though you might escape the terror of a moment, forever you will be remembered as traitors to your people."

Ama surveyed the guards, not a single sword dropped to the floor. Ama looked at Juria and nodded. "Queen Juria, command your guards."

Juria bowed to Ama then turned to the guards. "Guards of Acchora, know this. I do not mean to raise my sword to our people. They belong to us and we to them. I firmly believe that most remain loyal to Ama and her family, rightful rulers of the Drylings. We will fight Olmander if we must, but I propose that we flee. We must take as many loyal Drylings as we can with us above ground to fight the true war against our real enemy. I do not ask you to fight Drylings but to warn them. This mountain is about to shake again with fire. We must flee to safety. Olmander can take this underground kingdom. Let him push through that wall, and when he does, warn the people that the fire is about to erupt and that this mountain is no longer safe."

Juria turned from the guard and flew with Ama to the tree.

"Jill, it is time," she said. "You and Ama must leave. But first, you must do what the King requested. Jill, you must destroy the mountain."

Jill held the stone King Eckwith had given to her and looked at it carefully. "I can't believe I'm really going to do this. Where do we go from here, Ama?"

"As fast and far away from this mountain as possible, then toward Terador."

Jill took a deep breath and clenched her hand around the red stone. "I'm ready. Take me to the waterfall."

Juria bent down onto one knee. Jill sat between her wings and held onto her neck. In a burst of flight, three quick flaps of her wings, Juria had brought Jill to the waterfall. Ama hovered with them in the air.

"Fly to where the water falls out of the rock," Jill said. "That is where I must place the rock."

As the King instructed, Jill kissed the stone which was cold to the touch. When she removed it from her lips, the stone suddenly went hot and glowed so brightly that Jill had to close her eyes. Though it burned in her palm, Jill resisted dropping it. The pain in her hand slowly subsided and Jill opened her eyes. King Eckwith told Jill what to expect, but she was still astonished to see that the stone transformed into a tongue of fire that burnt in her open palm. She no longer felt any heat.

There was a loud noise behind them. The thick chamber door blocking Olmander from the entrance shattered, and Olmander crashed through with a group of Drylings weilding swords. Juria looked over her shoulder at Jill.

"Can't you throw the stone into the water yet, Jill? He's here, and we need to leave."

"Not yet, Juria. We must wait."

"What is she doing?" yelled Olmander. "Kill that sorceress. Don't you see she's trying to harm us?"

The royal guards hesitated and Olmander pushed passed them, leaving his companions to fight the defending guard. As he flew toward them, Juria handed Jill to Ama and turned to face her attacker.

"What do you plan to do, Juria? Force us out of the mountain?" asked Olmander in disbelief.

"It is what the King desired."

"Liar!" Olmander shouted and fell on Juria with his sword.

The force of Olmander's blow against Juria's sword thrust the two Drylings in a spinning arch toward the bottom of the waterfall. As they were falling, the tongue of fire in Jill's hand burst into a column of blinding white light. When the light from her hand filled the chamber so that it glowed with light, the fighting at the entrance stopped.

"We must flee the mountain," Juria shouted. "Flee!"

"Stop her!" Olmander shouted at his companions. "Stop her before she ruins the mountain with her black magic!"

"It is time," Ama said to Jill. "Do what my father commanded you to do."

Ama moved Jill so that she was inches away from the cascading water. Jill closed her eyes and thrust the hand that held the column of blinding light behind the waterfall, then quickly pulled her hand back. It was empty, but in the middle of her palm, Jill noticed her skin was branded with a very red mark. The stone and the light were gone!

The ground shook violently, throwing the Royal guards and Olmander's men to the ground; the cavern walls splintered and cracked. Juria's sword was still engaged in battle with Olmander's. The two Drylings flew at each other in mid air, swinging their weapons which sparked at each forceful blow.

"Juria, it is done!" Ama shouted. "We must flee."

"Olmander," Juria shouted between clashes of their swords, "we must leave." With that, she landed a blow against his back with the flat of her blade, knocking him out of the air. The old Dryling dropped his sword. "What is done is done, Olmander. Why are you so slow to see? You must now help our people flee to safety. You must help us assume our rightful place in our world."

"Never!" he gasped between breaths of air. "Never!"

"You are too stubborn for your own good. Come with us, Olmander. Leave this place, or it will be your grave."

"I cannot leave. I will not betray my people!" he said.

The ground shook again, with greater violence.

"Juria!" shouted Jill. "Move!"

Juria looked up to see the top of the waterfall transform from frothy water, to molten lava, orange as fire.

"Olmander, you old fool, come with me!"

"No!" he shouted, and dropped into the pool of water that collected at the bottom of the falls.

Juria turned and flew away with Jill and Ama, refusing to watch the old Dryling wait to be showered by the falling magma. The chamber continued to shake and great fissures broke open in the ground creating deep crevasses that would make it impossible to escape by foot. As Jill and Ama flew over the red stone path leading away from the King's tree toward the entrance, the path itself, once shining red stones, transformed into a dangerous path of liquid fire.

"Ama, look!" Jill shouted over the noise around her, pointing at the path.

"Yes Jill, soon the mountain itself will erupt. It has not done so for hundreds of years. We must flee."

*   *   *

283

Stelton, Tickthith, and Simon were thrown against the ground. The creature was nearly covered in his grave, but their progress was slow, since they could only use their hands.

"What was that?" Simon asked, as he found his feet when the shaking stopped and dusted dirt from his pants.

"It feels as though the whole chamber quaked," Tickthith said, looking at his master with concern.

"Does that happen a lot?" asked Simon.

"Very rarely," said Stelton.

"Well, what does it mean?"

"It's not good news. There is trouble in Acchora. The mountain is shaking. Ah!" he yelled, pulling his sword from his side and throwing it to the ground.

"Master, your sword!"

The blade lay against the ground, and on the hilt, the red stones burned brightly with fire.

"What is it?" Simon asked.

"My father," Stelton stuttered, "my father! He has found a way to activate the volcano! We need to find a way out of here. Quickly, cover his body. We must leave."

"How?" Tickthith asked. "These chambers will fill with fire too. The lava travels too fast. Perhaps it is right that we die with our people."

Simon stopped covering the creature with dirt and looked at Stelton.

"Die? Are we just going to sit here and wait to burn? I don't like the sounds of that."

"Nor do I, Simon. The Rashtakar's mirrors! Tickthith, we must find one that we can use."

"Master, they were all smashed."

"We thought there were no living Drylings down here either, Tickthith, but there were two. Let's search for a mirror. Simon, we'll be back shortly."

Before Simon could object, the Drylings had flown to the Rashtakar's cave and were searching among the shattered glass. Simon stepped back from the covered grave and was thrown from his feet by another violent tremor. When he hit the ground he landed sharply on his tail bone. Pain shot through his legs and back.

"The eggs!" Simon shouted, they had been jostled and were rolling away from the grave where Stelton had left them in his haste. Simon ran after them and carefully picked them off the ground. "No more death today, hey?" he whispered to them, "no more death."

When he looked back at the grave, he yelled in fright. A white, four fingered hand pointed out of the ground and shot high into the air. Perhaps the tremor had disturbed the grave, but no! As Simon looked, the arm continued to shoot into the air, higher and higher, the long white arm rose toward the roof. Suddenly, another arm thrust out of ground at a forty-five degree angle, then another, then another. Simon soon realized they weren't limbs of the creature, but the branches of a very white tree, that quickly burst from the ground.

Entire branches were now pushing up from the ground in long sweeping lines, like snakes rising to the surface of a lake. Simon had to jump out of the way of two branches as they shot up under his feet, throwing dirt and rock all around him like splashes of water. Simon heard a loud crack. A thick white tree trunk had already grown to the cavern ceiling and was starting to push its way through. A large crack formed along the span of ceiling and rock and stalactites began to fall.

"Stelton! Tickthith! In here! We're in trouble!" Simon shouted.

The Drylings turned from their search in the cave and looked at Simon.

"Simon!" yelled Stelton, who held a green gemstone. He tried to throw himself into the air to fly toward the boy, but even as he moved toward his young friend, a violent tremor knocked him off balance onto the floor. A sharp stalactite from the ceiling dropped and pierced his wing, pinning him to the ground. Tickthith flew to his aide, pulling with all his strength at the spearing rock that held his master against the ground.

Rock continued to fall and the tree continued to thrust through the ground. Simon pulled the eggs close to his body and said a prayer. A white branch flashed in front of his vision and he felt something hard hit the back of his head. As his sight slowly blurred, he heard an explosion of sound as the chamber wall crumbled and flames from the Dryling grave burst through the rock wall toward Stelton who was still pinned to the rock.

As he slowly slipped out of consciousness, Simon could see that Stelton reached out his hand as though to touch him, as though with one movement of his hand he could stop all the rock from falling and end the madness they found themselves thrown into. *So this is what it is like*, Simon found himself saying, no longer feeling weight in his body, feeling as though he left the ground and floated away. His friend fading further and further below him, arm still outstretched to Simon, now smiling, no longer gesturing with his hand to stop the rocks from falling, rather waving as if to say *goodbye, friend, have a pleasant journey of it*. Waving, perhaps hoping to see the young boy again.

*   *   *

The rush from the mountain through volcanic vents was a blur to Jill, full of screams and flapping wings and terrified voices. The mountain shook and heaved, its voice a voice of anger, fire the language of its wrath. Jill could feel heat against her skin from all directions. And the passage through darkness reminded her of another journey in a far away place that seemed like another life. A flight from her own home, one that was no longer safe, a home she never loved but lived in because that was where she was from. She held tightly to Ama's neck as she soared through the narrow volcanic vent, still empty of the molten enemy that pursued them, hundreds of winged Drylings frantically following behind their would-be Queen and the daughter of Grace who destroyed their home.

Jill closed her eyes and let the warm air rush over her cheeks, forcing herself not to gasp for

breath until she could breathe the cool air of
Acchora, that same feeling again, like she was
swimming for the surface of water after plunging
deeply into a black pool. Jill clutched the change
purse strung around her neck, full but for a single
coin that brought her to this world, and nine others,
now seeds, that compelled her onward to another.
Or was she chased? By men in her world who
would keep her from a life of magic and adventure.
By a voice that searched for her in the night. By fire
that would burn her to the bone.

"Breathe, Jill, we'll make it. I can see the light
of the sky." A new voice to fill the loneliness of
silence. "We're almost there. Breathe."

Jill opened her eyes at the sudden rush of cool
air against her cheeks, air that coaxed her to breathe
in the blueness of the sky. And when she opened her
eyes she remembered the softness of the clouds, and
had, for the first time in her life, something close
to a vision: a white tree that threw itself against the
sky, that grew taller than all the trees in the world.

Acknowledgements

THE AUTHOR WOULD LIKE TO
ACKNOWLEDGE THE COMMITTEE OF
THE LESZCZYNSKI/WALES WORSHIP
ARTS SCHOLARSHIP ISSUED BY
MEMBERS OF STREAMS CHURCH IN
RED DEER, ALBERTA:

About the Scholarship:

The Leszczynsk/Wales Worship Arts Scholarship was inspired by the lives and early passing of Henry Leszczynski and Kate Wales. It is given to create opportunity for people, both young and old, to experience and express worship in new ways, in the same spirit as Kate, whose desire was to creatively express her love for God.

Author Thanks:

Christopher Kooman — good eye. And all the others who helped along the way.

Other Work by Andrew Kooman:

THE GOSPEL WRITERS MEET:
Conversations with Saints Matthew, Mark, Luke and John

Andrew Kooman sits down with each of the Gospel writers for a series of candid interviews. Among other subjects, the Gospel writers discuss suffering, meaning in language, the Gospel, their personal poetics, cyborgs, and the apocalypse. Filled with fresh dialogue, some of their newest poems, and surprising turns of thought, the Gospel writers are back at their game of surprise and inspiration.

30 DAYS OF PRAYER FOR THE VOICELESS

Filled with moving pictures and facts about issues of Gender Based Injustice as well as fourteen original short stories by Andrew Kooman. Be part of the growing movement by reading the booklet that has been translated into Japanese, Korean, German, Urdu, Russian, Spanish and other languages. With a foreword by Loren Cunningham.

NAZAR

The celebrated short story, winner of the 2004 Hobson Prize for fiction. A young Canadian college student tutors Nazar, a refugee from Afghanistan, in English. Unable to communicate with each other beyond basic words and signs, the young man tries to piece together the story of Nazar's flight from the Taliban, through Pakistan into Canada.

WISDOM FOR EVERYDAY LIVING

The creative and thought-provoking study booklet that examines the nature of wisdom, God's view of love, friendship, wealth, and godly living. The booklet includes questions study groups can ask to generate discussion, and action points to help bring the wisdom of the proverbs to life.

Download or purchase these and more exciting works at:

www.andrewkooman.com

The following is a Sneak Peak at the second book in Jill Strong's adventures.

FROM
TEN SILVER COINS:
THE JOURNEY TO TERADOR
BY ANDREW KOOMAN

*   *   *

"Drylings keep moving!"
  Ama's voice ripped through the noise of wind rushing over wings, the roaring sound of the volcano, the panicked murmur of Drylings fleeing for their lives in the deep and dark passage of the mountain's rock.
  "The mountain will soon erupt. Fly! Fly!" Jill was astonished at the power and clarity of the beautiful Queen's voice in the midst of all the madness, sure it, like the volcano dormant and silent for years, could be stopped or silenced by no power now that it's time to be heard had come.

Jill looked above from where she was held secure, tucked under Ama's arm. She could see a rim of light in the distance slowly growing bigger like a shining orb, slowly eclipsing the surrounding darkness. Behind her was the sound of the other Drylings and the volcano.

"We're nearly there. Quickly!"

And suddenly all went white. Jill squinted her eyes shut at the sudden blinding light. They were out of the mountain! The fresh air of Acchora hit her lungs and she drank in air violently.

"Higher! Higher Drylings! Out of the volcano's reach!"

They climbed higher and higher in the sky. The pressure of the climb forced Jill's head downward against her chest. Black spots interrupted her vision of a spectacular sight: hundreds of Drylings, some holding their young closely to their chests pumping their wings in strong, determined movements, higher and higher above the sunken dome of the volcano. Still other Drylings were emerging out of the different tunnelled lava tubes, desperately willing themselves and their loved ones against the force of gravity in fear of the liquid fire.

Jill suddenly felt weightless as her upward movement toward the sky ceased, though her heart and stomach seemed to keep moving. She looked up to see Ama's wings arched across the sky like an enormous leathery parachute.

"We've climbed far enough," Ama yelled so all around her could hear. "We should be out of danger now. Use the current from the sea to stay at this height."

All around them other Drylings unfurled their wings against the sky, ending their desperate climb to catch the warm wind Jill could feel against her skin. Everyone around Jill and Ama looked toward the volcano, watching, urging the other Drylings toward them.

Before Jill could join in their urgent calls for the others, the air all around Jill was filled with a hot rush. Her skin burned with the sudden onslaught of heat as though she had been thrown into an invisible fire. The earth seemed to howl with the rage. The afternoon sky lit up with an orange flash.

The volcano!

The Drylings around her screamed at the shock of it. The heat seared against Jill's skin as the sky lit up with terrible orange fire. And the sound. Jill covered her ears at the sound, a deep rumbling growl as the volcano spewed, like some deep sinister evil were laughing and yelling in a chorus of fury.

And then, just as suddenly there was a great hush. For a moment, after all the frantic flying and the desperate climb to the sky, the noise and shrieks through the mountain, everything was quiet. The terrible belch of lava seemed to stop its terrible orange arc against the sky. Jill and the Drylings were caught in a moment of silent horror.

Jill's had felt this sensation before. For a moment she felt as though she were in The Music Room again, the earth-shaking tremor of the bass woofer charging through her heart like a stampede, suddenly suspended in the air. Caught by surprise, completely out of control. But as the heavy cloud of ash started to descend upon her and the creatures around her, Jill was all too aware that this was not some beautiful chorus being played somehow in the far reaches of her girlish imagination. This was a symphony of destruction and it was very likely Drylings had been swallowed by the mountain.

"Jill, look at me, look away from the fire. It will blind you," Ama shouted over the sound into Jill's ear.

"Ama, the ash. It burns!"

"I know. We must all leave. The mountain will not rest until it has purged itself of all its rage."

Jill looked at her friend, terrified.

"We'll be safe," Ama said, "but not here. We must move."

*   *   *

To be continued...

Visit

www.tensilvercoins.com

for exciting new content and all the latest Jill
Strong news